"YOU MUST BE THE CHANGE YOU
WISH TO SEE IN THE WORLD."

-GANDHI

"THE BEAUTIFUL THING ABOUT
LEARNING IS NOBODY CAN TAKE IT
AWAY FROM YOU."

-B.B KING

OPEN THE GATES
PRESENTS

DIED DOIN' DIRTY WORK:

FROM THE DUMP

A NOVEL BY:

JOSH GATES

Open The Gates, LLC

OpenTheGatesLLC@gmail.com

ABOUT THE AUTHOR

Artist Josh Gates has previously been signed to Universal Republic Records for his first single "Look Back At It", worked with YMCMB, and most recently worked independently with Kevin Gates on "WYND" and "Talk A Lil Shit". All Josh's independent albums include Battling Myself, 24:15, and Open The Gates can be found on Spotify, iTunes, and all other digital music outlets. During 2010 and 2011, Josh's acting career landed him roles in films played on HBO, Starz, Fox, and Lifetime which can be credited in the movies Carjacked, The Mortician, and Blood Out.

In 2014, Josh was incarcerated in Louisiana and is currently finishing out his sentence. At the beginning of Josh's incarceration, he was forced to slow down from his fast lifestyle and with a sober mind he was able to reflect; writing his first true life movie script. Imagine the life of a young artist and actor, drug dealer and addict, lover and father describing events, opportunity, and what it is like growing up in the industry. Soon after, Josh started writing the first novel to his book series "Died Doin' Dirty Work". This book series expresses Josh's true talent and will leave his readers eager to read the next book. Each story is packed with action, relatable characters, and takes a deeper look into the lives of those who live through hard times.

OPEN THE GATES

WHAT'S AVAILABLE NOW:

Music by Josh Gates include the following albums:

Open The Gates

Battling Myself

24:15

WHAT'S COMING NEXT:

Part II of Died Doin' Dirty Work: Team-13

The Silent Theaters: Modern Day Dictatorship

CHAPTERS:

DUMP ESCAPE

Jail time. Hard time. Everyday inmate shit, in a max prison. One specific inmate, that been going through it on the inside and outside, literally. Has been getting maxed out. Especially time wise, he's always been looking for a perfect route out. He found one on this day. But it led to him running for the rest of his life. He's not going back.

A man jumps a tall fence with bob wire on top. A guard see's him and quickly chases him, but he's so fast through the yard. He's moving and jumping like he's possessed. The guard calls for backup, but he jumps the last fence. He's at the top stuck in bob wire as the other guards come with their guns drawn. He flips through the bob wire forward, catches on to part of the fence, and hit the ground hard. They wanna shoot, but he's not moving for a few seconds. He's so close to freedom, he thinks so. He crawls, get up limp and keep going, but backup is everywhere now.

Close by the jail is a courthouse with police and workers everywhere, and his description is quickly out and broadcasted. He now needs a better plan, and a weapon fast or he's getting got. He sees a squad car in the back of the courthouse with a cop loading up. Further to the right is a patrol car that rides around making sure everything's okay all day. He walks up behind the cop drawing the gun from his waist, hits him, and drags him to the front of the squad car. Then, snap the cuffs on him to the steering wheel, beats the cop and tells him to call all units, and say he went another route and everything's clear. The cop had another thing in mind, so his mind was blown off in the car.

Changing his shirt was the only change since they wear regular jeans and shoes. He slid into a t-shirt. Still with the gun tucked, he went to the other patrol car. Put the gun to him and said, "Get in the car and get me the safest route out of here." The patrol guy ain't want no trouble. He already got the news earlier about the escapee. The only way to get this inmate out of his life without ending in a shootout, with his life at risk, was "FROM THE DUMP."

Driving towards the front gate seemed like the best plan, at first. But now, so much tension was up because all backup was on alert. They refused to let a prisoner out smart them with guards at the prison, and the courthouse on standby already. As the driver was getting to a check point before the gate, he quickly turned the car around.

The inmate felt it was a setup and pushed the gun towards him. The patrolee, that didn't want any trouble, said, "There's a safer way out. I can go around the back and drop you through the dump. It goes through a machine that has only one guard at the end. That makes sure everything was compressed legal and illegal, of course. If you get by him, you're back on the streets in no time."

This dump was hard metal inside and around. It didn't look big enough to fit a body, large amounts of drugs, packages of foods, and electronic items. However, he instantly knew it was a gold mine but as of right now getting out safe was first on the list. Sliding down the dump, which look like a playground slide that could end up in being chopped up and compressed if you didn't get out in time, seemed like it was never going to end. A guard was at the end before the chopping blocks; eating. If he gets past him it might be it, but what the patrolee didn't say was it was at the bottom of the 3-story courthouse. He still had to make it out the door unnoticed. Damn another plan.

"Maybe I can get outta this alive. I know the things I did before, in the system, out and in. They'll take me out. I gotta beat the system, but if I don't, at least I made it out the dump."

Died Doin' Dirty Work: From the Dump

VISIT DAY

(Reflection)

It's Tuesday, everybody getting fly haircuts, shaving, and showering. Seem like it's a big day. Well in the joint; it is. It's visit day, but man this visit day ain't regular. It's like no other. You see, every jail facility is different. Some have visits, some don't. Some have contact visits, but some only have glass visits. But with the best warden ever heard of in the system, once a month you can get scheduled a real contact visit. So, the reason why today is so special, because a few people have visits set up. Some guys want a chance to score. Just touch pussy, fuck some pussy, or even smell some pussy. Some guys even want to go further and get contraband. Every chance is risky, but knowing if you score in any way; you're the man especially if you rarely make store. You won't have to worry about making store. You can make your own prices, and fill your locker up. Everyone looks for one person to be successful.

Flint is called to get ready for visit. Nervous, but ready. He hasn't seen his girl in forever. She's straight up with it. They set up a plan, talked about it in code, and now the show must go on. Man, did she wear what she was supposed to wear. Did she bring what she's supposed to. From the locked door, he can see her clearly. No nervous in her, but all the butterflies in the world in him. If the talk and plan can go right, freedom can be soon.

Finally, the door opens courtesy of a big fat guard who only is worried about eating and checking out his girl. Hugs and kisses are the first words shared. Love has been there and never left, no matter how many miles have been in between. Straight to the point he said, "Baby, we only have about 30 to 45 minutes, so this must go smooth. I think I have a way out now. Remember I was telling you about Mike."

Mike grew up in the heart of the 17th ward. Him and Flint been at this thing called life. Coming up they hit licks together, sold dope together, fucked bitches together, even caught there first body together (two years earlier). Money was low, dog food (heroin) wasn't moving like they need it to, and they took a hit for some broad that owns clothing stores throughout the city. Her brother was in a bind, locked up upstate, and the rat was gonna be testifying against him. So, she reached out to Flint, who was fucking her on the regular, and gave him the mission. It was only ten racks, but what the hell, they needed the money bad. Mike was with it and they got him outta there. Everything went smooth and it was a success, but some months down the line, the murder came up because of phone records. Because Flint was fucking Monica, she was reckless with phone calls, and messages to his main cell line. Because it was his first time murking something, he was reckless how he went by doing it. The laws picked up Monica first since she was the planner, and the only other person they had anything on, was Flint. But about the time they went looking for him. He had gotten the news that a warrant was out for his arrest, for the murder of James Blanchard, and he went on the run instantly.

Leaving the city, he gave Mike his loyalty. If anything happens to where he gets caught, he's staying silent. "So, you don't have to worry, hide, or run. Just make sure if that do happen, hold me down through it." When they hit the trap spot in the 17th, they rounded up a few junkies and they caught Mike on some drug charges, but still no Flint. The Detective on the case was determined to catch Flint Myers, because the crime rate was too high, and jobs was on the line. Police Chief Jim Smith was ready for The National Guard, FEDS, government, and anybody from around the world. To help solve the killing problem in New Orleans.

In every city, state, town, country, or jail facility; you have rats. So, on that trap spot round up, one of the junkies mentioned the Westbank Apartments, that Flint crashes at when not trapping. Not giving no leads, Flint wasn't there. He was already on I-10 west, heading to the small country town where family live, New Roads.

After two days of hiding out, no real money, and family even threating to rat him out. He planned for the take down. Spending five racks on lawyer Ken Miles and having words with his lover, Serenity, he turned himself in. Awaiting trial, him and Monica stayed in contact through mail. Never talking about the case, but in code how they gonna be strong. Meaning take their own lick, and of course, not leaking their affair out to his girl. The only help he was receiving was from Serenity, and she was gonna ride to the end.

The only problem was, the end was very near, with Monica pleading guilty to accessory (twenty years suspended five) aggravated. Flint pleaded to 1st degree murder, a mandatory life sentence, no possibility of parole eligibility. Mike took a plea deal on his first drug charge and got five years' probation. He skipped a whole murder rap, but his loyalty must up hold now, more than ever.

Back at the Parish jail, where Flint was housed for the last two years, now twenty years old. He knew he would be shipped soon after taking his time. With the plan from Mike, and a contact visit for Tuesday visit day, he is more than sure he will not spend the rest of his life in a prison.

Mike didn't have the money to joce Flint the two years he was down, but he made sure to answer the phone and setup a fake ID and passport. Flint stayed in contact with people he knew he'll need one day, on the outside. One in particular was a hot young rapper, Dez, from Ghana. They met in the streets of Atlanta. Flint traveled anywhere a rental car could get him. Mike went on most road trips with him. They setup shop anywhere, especially when something hot was in town. Dez and his crew was in Hotlanta for the hip hop awards, and like young guys, they needed bud. Flint and Mike was in town with the works. They exchanged numbers and got real kool. Dez started telling him about behind the scenes of music, where all their gold and jewelry came from. A big trade out in Africa; gold bars, cars, diamonds, laptops, iPhones, and anything of value worth some big bucks.

Died Doin' Dirty Work: From the Dump

FLINT'S FIRST TAKE AFTER ESCAPE

Being that Flint kept contact with Dez and learned the trade game. All he needed was some good items. His team was small and tight already; his girl, Serenity, and Mike. Mike's job was to get guns and other accessories needed in a take. Serenity was in charge of having accounts setup. Making sure money was good, basically, the smarts behind the scenes. Flint was good with getting jobs done, but a loyal team made him that much better.

When Flint escaped from St. Landon jail, he kept all contact info from the patrolee that told him about the dump. He threatened officer Willer Agnes with his driver's license info that if he put him in any danger or bind his family would be payed visits until all of them were dead. Who wouldn't believe a man that just escaped from jail wouldn't do it. Not only did he get the officer's info. He got a cell number and house number, because if he knew about the dump; he would know what time officers make visits and when there's a large bust. No telling what kind of merchandise, drugs, or money would be going down there. No telling what crooked city official goes there; the governor, mayor, police squad. Hell, maybe the President is even in on that joint.

Not even a full two days after escaping, Flint contacted Officer Agnes on his cell phone from a prepaid number. Agnes answered and was shocked to learn that the escapee was still alive. Flint got straight to the business, "Yo Agnes, you remember that dump you told me go down? Well I made it thru, as you can tell." Flint made it out before the crushing. Even though he didn't see any merchandise, he did see broken up particles all at the bottom of the dump, electronic wires, and could smell raw coke and burnt money. If he'd escaped a day earlier, he probably would've caught the dump. But greed would've got him either killed or hauled back off to jail.

The only thing Agnes was thinking was even if Flint made it out the dump, how did he make it out the courthouse and pass the officers? If Agnes would've watched the news, he would've known. But being he took a leave after the horrific events that left him scared for his safety and the safety of his family; Agnes didn't know much. The only thing he would be updated with was whenever their scanner beeped three times which meant it was a major bust or a drop off. That would be the only thing Flint is interested in knowing. Fuck the wellbeing of him and his family.

Flint said the next words calm, "When is the next dump?" Agnes haven't gotten any news of anything happening. So, he was truthful and said, "Once my scanner sends me a signal, I can inform you." Flint thought he was playing on his top and said, "You know I have your address." Agnes said, "Please be patient. I'll contact you as soon as I get word. I'll let you know who all will be there, and if it's even worth the risk." For some reason, Flint felt the man being sincere and thought he'll let him live; for now at least.

Hanging up the phone, Flint thought about how after he got out the dump. How he jammed the gun into the waiting officer side. Made him strip, get in the dump. Then he put on his police uniform and hat and walked out the courthouse bottom floor. Fuck if he got crushed.

That night around nine o'clock p.m. Officer Agnes hit up Flint and said, "The dump is tonight. It's quick. It will be four officers."

They hit what they thought was a meth lab in Slidell, but come to find out, it was another dirty job. That the five officers usually do undercover after their regular shifts in the city. Agnes didn't have all the info since he wasn't there on the lick, but he did speak with one of his buddies to know what they found in the lab.

The white hippies that the officers had been watching come in and out the city, buying different items from chemistry labs, electronics from Best Buy, and driving back to Slidell to a Twin Spain Subdivision. They wondered how hippies lived in such a lavish home, and what was in the tinted glass house that sat in the back. Well come to find out, when the officers illegally hit the house. They found out it was no meth lab, and that the items they watched purchase, was for experimenting the make of new pills. The officers cut a dirty deal with the Slidell Police. To where, after they ran in and took everything; they planted meth, called the Slidell Police, and a warrant was served. The crooked shit cops do seem to surpass the everyday neighborhood crimes. The four dirty officers seized two hundred and fifty thousand dollars out the lavish home. Along with what looked like over ten thousand homemade x pills, five new iPhones, and ten Apple laptops; five in the home and five in the glass house. Instantly the scanner beeped three times and that's how Agnes got in on the take. Officer Agnes gave Flint the whole rundown. The car they would be in, the route they took, etc.

Flint had Mike get a rental van and two guns with silencers. They would change the plate, and wear painted masks. Mike would be the driver, dressed like a woman, and since Flint grew dreads his two years down. He shaved his normal full beard, he wore since seventeen years old, and pinned his dreads up under a baseball cap.

On cue just as planned, a black Dodge Challenger exited the I-10 interstate onto a dark side street two blocks from the jail. Mike had the van parked under the bridge exit. Flint was laid in the back not able to see in the tinted-out Challenger. Mike pulled behind and rammed into the Challenger. To his surprise, only two undercovers exited the vehicle. The plan was gonna work even better now.

As they approached what looked like a female driver, they didn't have their straps drawn. A sliding door on the right, and a sliding driver side window. Whispered, two silenced shots to the head. They put the two bodies in the van. Flint drove the Challenger under the bridge following Mike in the van. They changed into the officers' undercover clothes, put them in black bags, and laid them on the back seats of the Challenger. Flint drove the dark street to B Lane, the same route the officers were taking, until they came up to the gate behind the courthouse.

One buzz from the remote in the car and they were inside like a normal routine the officers always did. Before they checked the vehicle for their big payoff, Flint plan was to get rid of the bodies, and because he traveled through the dump on his escape from St. Landon. He knew, two lifeless bodies, would be chopped and crushed to unidentified pieces by morning. Flint told him to check the car fully before they threw the bodies, and good thing they did, because what seemed like thousands of pills was about to be in the bags with them, upon discovery.

Mike hated the idea of getting rid of the drugs; he seen the smaller picture. Flint wasn't trying to small hustle; he was really on the run. Everything had to be big enough and worth it to survive without getting caught. The black duffle bag had a lot of cash. Too much to count at that moment, and the big brown moving box had all kinds of electronics in it. Happy as shit while throwing the bodies down the dump. It was time for Flint to call Dez and Serenity.

Those cops died doin' dirty work.

Died Doin' Dirty Work: From the Dump

THE MOVE TO CALI

(Breaking News) Two St. Landon police officers were found shot to death, down in the bottom of the courthouse terminal which is used for legal seizures. Found on the officers, were thousands of pills. Head Chief Jim Smith says, "It's an investigation going on at this time...."

Flint and Serenity took a flight out of Armstrong Airport first thing the next morning to LAX. The breaking news was hard to miss, waiting to board the plane. Thanks to Flint's new look, and the fake ID and passport Mike setup for him. The couple blended in like every other citizen taking a flight. Mike's flight was scheduled for that evening. He was to fly into Burbank, California and with a quick drive in a rental car; they'll all be reunited in no time.

The night before Flint and Mike had drove the Challenger back under the bridge, loaded the van up, set the car on fire, and drove out to Kenner. Close by the airport, to the Sleep Inn. Nothing fancy, just somewhere to count the money in the duffle bag, and get thoughts processed on what's next. Only counting the money and not touching the box, from it being too big and noticeable. They quickly noticed it wasn't a quarter mill, like Agnes had told Flint, it was one hundred and twenty-five thousand dollars.

The first call went to Agnes, and Flint found out that instead of four officers, it was only two. The other two took their half of the pot and split up. Since nothing never went wrong on the scheming before, they trusted each other with their word. The two officers that was in route to the dump was supposed to chop and crush all evidence, pills, and electronics. Keep the cash, meet back up, and celebrate. But as Agnes finished talking, he knew the real celebration was for Flint. Flint had told Agnes, one day he'll be working for him instead of the law.

The second call went to Dez out in Ghana. The rapper had not only reached success in Africa but was getting "Nominations in America." Flint told him that he had some new gadget items he hasn't fully checked out yet, but from the looks of 'em they're pretty new. Dez told Flint, he was up for an award in California for the BET Awards in a few days. Him and his team would be arriving early to get acquainted with the city. That was enough for a move to Cali and with the info to the hotel and reservations; the third call was to Serenity.

Serenity had been living alone for the past two years in their apartment on the Westbank. She took over while Flint was down and while working a in home job for Humana. She only did online college classes and waited for Flint's calls. She yearned for the day they can have a family, and a fairytale life. Answering the phone barely asleep, she looked at the clock that showed eleven o'clock p.m. She instantly thought he was in some kind of bind. Being that he couldn't go home with the laws out for his arrest after escaping. They haven't had alone time in years. She missed his touch, and he missed hers. He gave her a quick run down on the nights events and gave her the move for the morning.

Not believing the events really happened, she was just excited to be in a foreign city together with her man. Rich or poor; she just wanted to be free with him. The three-and-a-half-hour flight to Cali was over quick being that it was Flint and Serenity's first time flying, ever. They did it like naturals. Flint had traveled by rental car through the south, but Serenity had never been passed Texas, and that was during Hurricane Katrina. Neither of them had been to the West Coast.

With a limo waiting at the airport and a driver with the sign "Caters" waiting on them down the escalators. Them and their carry on was off to checking into the SLS Beverly Hills. Being that Flint was on the run and even though he had a fake ID and passport, he put everything in Serenity Caters name. They needed to shop, buy all new things, and rent a car for personal moves. Just riding in the back of the stretched black limo, Serenity was ready to ask Flint to live in the star-studded city for good.

Upon arrival to the hotel, they thought they had died and went to heaven. It was beautiful. Outside by valet, people dressed up like a ball was every day. As you're walking up the stairs to the lobby by check-in, there were white leather plush seating areas. A restaurant awaits you to your right, serving anything from shrimp and grits to steak and lobster. While Serenity was checking in, Flint was admiring the solid glass walls by the elevators. On one side, you can go to certain floors. But on the other side, you can go higher to the penthouse suites. Their reservation was for a presidential suite. It had an all-white setting with a Jacuzzi, glass mirrors all around, a view that overlooked the city, and the main attraction was the bathroom. You can push the glass to walk in through the bathroom. Some James Bond type shit. Of course, Serenity was obsessed with the bathroom, she got her girly girl on. It was in that moment, Flint noticed how much he missed and loved the 5'6, 140-pound, light skinned girl. She had a face like the GiGi Hadid girl, eyes like Rihanna, but thick like Amber Rose. Her hair was black, down the middle of her back, with red streaks through it.

Sitting on the leather couch, he got hard thinking about all the time he was locked down. The contact visit day and the recent time he been on the run and haven't filled her tight walls with his long thick dick. He watched her thru the open glass to the bathroom take off her t-shirt and jogging tights she'd flown in. She started playing in her hair while running the bath water. Flint slid out his basketball shorts and V-neck, showing his muscles and tattoos. Dimmed the lights, walked up behind Serenity, and started kissing her back. Soft kisses up to her neck, back down to each one of her cheeks. Down the back of her legs, then slid her thong off. She was so stuck, she never turned around. He tasted her pussy from the back. Ummm tastes like morning. He stuck his tongue in her hole, a gasp for breath tried to escape her mouth, but once he turned her around. He set her up on the sink and ate the pussy like groceries. He sucked her pearl and licked her pearl until she shook. He kept eating her, and she kept saying, "Lo Lo Lo Lo." He payed it no mind until she started hitting his back and pointing to the water about to over flow. He cut the water off.

Picked her up, walked through the glass opening, to the king size bed. Then filled her wet warming, with dick that she been yearning for. It was so tight when the head pushed in. He felt himself go in a different layer, and about the time he was halfway inside her, his dick was curving up in her. She came a second time, before the dick was all the way in. Once from eating the pussy, and once from inserting the head. After fucking her in four different positions, he finally came on cue with her third. He exploded like the levees broke again. They both got in the jacuzzi. Held each other, kissed, and had a moment of peace and quietness.

Counting money from the take, the night before. Flint kept one hundred thousand dollars and gave Mike twenty-five thousand dollars. Just until he arrived in Cali. Mike was the same age as Flint, but more young minded, so it was best that way. Flint thought twenty-five racks was too much, leaving with him alone in New Orleans. Flint and Serenity pulled the five iPhones and ten laptops out of each of their carry-ons. To have them ready for Dez's arrival, later that week.

Right now, it was time to shop and see the city. After eating ordered room service shrimp, steak, and potatoes. They had about six hours, before having to pick up Mike from the Burbank airport. Serenity rented a Chrysler 300 from the airport. After they finished shopping, the limo would take them to pick up the vehicle, and just be on call to their every need while on their trip.

Serenity wanted all the latest fashion she had been behind on and haven't even seen before going to Cali. They hit up Rodeo Drive and got jewelry. Serenity got an ankle bracelet, tennis bracelet, and a heart shaped necklace. All white gold set, with diamonds, for ten thousand dollars. Flint purchased a small gold cross necklace, and a gold bracelet with diamonds, for five thousand dollars. He wasn't big on watches. After hitting Melrose and the Beverly Center. They spent ten thousand dollars on red bottoms, Jordans, custom made dresses, True Religion, Gucci, and Louis Vuitton. Serenity got her hair fixed in curls, at one of the salons. Flint didn't spend money on his, because Serenity would twist and braid his dreads, neat back at the hotel.

While Serenity was getting her hair done. Flint made a call to Mike, to make sure everything was straight, and he was ready to make the three-and-a-half-hour flight. When Mike didn't answer, he left a message. He tried calling back two more times, but still no answer. Now worried, he had no choice but to play it by ear and hope Mike didn't do anything stupid. Maybe he's gather up his things, maybe he's rushing, maybe even getting some pussy before heading out. After talking to Serenity about Mike not answering. While in route to pick up the rental car, the phone rang. It was an unfamiliar number, but since the escape no one had access to the prepaid phone; except Agnes, Dez, Mike, and Serenity. Answering the phone, Flint learned that Mike was back in jail, and the events that led to it was what Flint was scared of.

MIKE'S TIME

Instead of Mike going home to that big butt bitch, Reba, from the East and getting some pussy before flying out. He decided to go to Little Darlings on Bourbon Street. A fucking strip club with ten thousand dollars cash on him, and pills he took from the trunk of the Challenger. Instead of throwing all the pills in the dump with the officers, he kept a stash for profit and pleasure.

Flint learned that Mike was drinking, throwing twenties at bitches, popping x pills, giving x pills to the strippers, and the girls were selling them to customers. Tricking them out their money, getting them high, and not giving them no pussy. Well one unsatisfied customer got heated after not getting no ass for cash and ratted the what seemed like organized crime out to the street police. What was supposed to be a night of living like a hood king for Mike, turned to be a police raid. With what seemed like the whole police department, running in the one way in, one way out strip club. Owners, strippers, bartenders, and customers were arrested. Mike's charges were PWIT narcotics and probation violation. He was scheduled to meet his PO the next morning, to piss test before his flight out, but now none of those events would happen.

All Flint could do is shake his head in disbelief and tell Mike he'll have Serenity set up their paid lawyer, Ken Miles, and get him the best turnout he can possibly get. Flint didn't cut no corners, he told him the real, "This is your second drug charge while on supervised five-year probation. You will do some time, but we can hope for something light." He told Mike give him till tomorrow, and the lawyer would be up to St. Landon to see him. They said, "Loyal to my brother" then hung up the phone. All Flint could think about was, why he didn't keep a closer look out on Mike before the flight, and what the hell happened to the other fifteen thousand dollars out the twenty-five thousand dollars he was given that night. So many other questions passed his brain also, but right now he needed Serenity to make that call to their paid lawyer, and he needed some Kali

Kush to mellow him out after these past two days of events.

After talking with the lawyer, Mike knew he had to serve some time. So, he was prepared for what was in front of him. Thank God, he got caught up on the drugs and violation, and not the bodies. At this point, he was in on three murders, and never caught up on one. Flint was unlucky, he's running for the rest of his life, from being loyal. In court, the same courthouse Mike and Flint disposed two dirty officers' bodies in. Judge Treme sentenced Mike Aime to five years. Because it was a non-violent crime he had to serve only forty percent of the five years, and with a year of good time from taking classes. He would be set to hit the streets again in about eighteen months. Flint received the news from Mike and wanted to come up with a good plan to keep both of them eating, especially since Flint and Serenity were now living in Cali. Flint also learned that Mike stashed the other fifteen thousand dollars at Reba's house. He did go get him some pussy before hitting the strip club. After all, with Reba putting money on his books and jocing him, that would give Flint time to put things together while Mike was on his short stay.

Mike got adjusted to his cell after the first couple of months. He missed his freedom. He missed pussy. But most of all he knew he was supposed to be in Cali enjoying the weather, the beaches, the money, the bitches, and basically a new life with Flint. But here he was, locked up with a celly, over some stupid shit he could've avoided. Once a week, he talked to Flint to check on things and plans, he could always tell Flint was a little troubled. The calls would be kool, but he talked about the price of living being high and surviving off the cash from the first take. Money was always going down, instead of being added to. Even though some of that money belonged to Mike also, Mike understood Flint needed it more. He was on the run and he always came through. Shit if it wasn't for Flint, they'll probably be both doing life right this moment, but they always kept high hopes and a plan was in the making. Flint had thought somethings over, and a call to Agnes was in the making. With

Agnes back at work and Mike locked up in St. Landon, some moves would be made.

FLOODING ST. LANDON

After beneficial talks with Officer Agnes. He was able to set Mike up with a job at the courthouse, cleaning up. Flint convinced Agnes to bring in ounces of mojo, ounces of good California weed, and flip cell phones. Agnes couldn't turn it down for two reasons; his life depended on it and he couldn't do those dirty jobs. Being that, two of his fellow officers died doin' dirty work. That still was unsolved, and the dump was now heavily guarded around the clock surveillance cameras. A guard outside and inside to watch every drop carefully. His lavish lifestyle of living was put on hold and being a police officer wasn't making the big payoff.

Once the plan was in motion. Flint told Agnes, "I knew you'll be working for me someday, just was sooner than planned." Getting good prices on mojo and California weed was no problem. The shipping wasn't even a problem. Agnes had a vacant rental home, he'll have Flint mail the goods packaged tight in cereal boxes, with different names on the packages. Flint was paying three hundred dollars for two ounces in Cali. Down south that's the price for one. The normal profit would be about fourteen hundred dollars. But in the jail market, that tripled to around forty-two hundred dollars a week, off of mojo and kush alone. Since Flint did business with Dez, on the iPhones and laptops. He turned around and got a favor from him. A hundred cheap flip phones sent from Ghana, at ten dollars each, was going for a hundred dollars each in jail. They only made ten thousand dollars off of phones that first six months, but the real money was coming from the smoke. Everybody couldn't afford phones, plus the risk was higher to get caught. But the whole jail wanted smoke on demand. They paid in money transfers, Paypal, and Green Dots. The only time Mike would bring in a package, was when Agnes shift was on at the courthouse. He would never be searched. He basically walked in the jail with at least an ounce of mojo, an ounce of kush, and a couple of cell phones. That was faithfully once a week, for a whole year of Mike's stay at St. Landon.

Flint cut Agnes a deal, of twenty percent, of everything coming in. Serenity ran the numbers, she had the accounts set up for money transfers, and an account for Mike savings upon his release. Everything was organized and ran smoothly. If someone would've tipped off the warden. Mike's celly, Coren, would plug the contraband. Flint made sure his commissary stayed full also, because of his bravery, of making sure the operation ran smoothly. No one was being too greedy, and everyone was eating. That year, they grossed one hundred eighty-four thousand and seven hundred twenty dollars. Putting up eighty-four thousand seven hundred and twenty dollars for Mike coming home gift. Flint was one hundred thousand dollars up, after being down to his last twenty-five thousand after their first take.

Flint and Serenity was living very normal. In a Hollywood studio apartment off of Sunset, for fifteen hundred a month. Not luxury, but location meant everything. Survival and spending money wisely, was now the only plan, until the only person Flint truly trusted came home. Up until the flooding St. Landon profit, they rented cars to get around, and switching them every week. Flint decided to let Serenity pick their first luxury car. A white 3 series Beamer, fresh off the lot, for thirty thousand dollars. It was a beauty. Fully loaded, black leather seats, wood grain dash, glass top with sunroof, tinted windows, push start, custom wheels, automatic. Easy for Serenity to drive. They also purchased a Bersa 380. In Serenity name, with a mini drum that holds twenty-two rounds. It was the safety that Flint needed. They lived a very private life. He didn't want to be slipping with a Hollywood pad, a brand-new Beamer, and no heat while still on the run.

With six months left to Mike's stay at St. Landon, it was time for Flint to start making plans for the team. Where would Mike live? He'll be off of paper and done with his time. What would he do with his part of the money? They couldn't be in the streets selling dope. They could, but that'll make the wanted man Flint hot, and that's the one thing they been avoiding

Dez always said Mike had the look of a rap artist. When Flint and Mike was young, they always played with the idea of being like a Puffy and Biggie, or Baby and Lil Wayne. Mike would spit, and Flint would dance like Diddy and do hand rubs like Baby at the same time. Some funny shit, they never were serious, especially since all they grew up knowing was nickel and dime hustling. One week while on a call with Mike, he wanted to see where his head was at. Flint asked Mike, "Do you think you have what it takes to make it in the rap game?" A shocking response from Mike, almost made Flint drop the phone. Mike started spitting with a slur like he grew up in prison, calling himself "MIC-AIM". He told Flint he been practicing, but never mentioned it, because their situation and it was a pipe dream.

HEAD TARGET

Instantly hanging up the phone with Mike, Flint got the picture so clear. He can make money in the music business legally, and still be behind the scenes to avoid heat drawn to him. With a call to Dez, he needed to know everything about the industry he can learn. Even though Dez was from Ghana, the same rules must apply. Flint thought, since Dez was getting nominations here, like he was from here. They had to be doing something right.

Over the next few months, Flint was soaking in the music game. He stayed in contact with Dez, finding out they record on pro tools. He wanted the studio setup. He felt, he could make Mike slow down a bit, by keeping him in a studio recording. He had Serenity do all the research on copyrights, LLC, PR work, etc. He had one big problem to work out. Who would run the company for him? Of course, he would have things in Serenity's name, but he couldn't go out to public outings in the spot light. He understood his position in this life was to, enjoy the lavish life, but he had to stay off the radar by all means. Flint laid it down for Dez, he'd make him CEO of "Head Target" in the states. He had his own funding. He wouldn't get in his overseas music business. This would work out for Dez also, because even though he was nominated and visiting the states often. This would put him here permanent, and all artist want a piece of America. You haven't made it, unless you're a household name in the states. Since Dez's family was over his music career in Ghana, they saw the bigger picture, and the dollar signs. Dez would be more in charge of blowing up Mike here in the states, instead of himself. That was his only concern, him taking a seat back behind Mike.

Flint was straight up with him and said, "It's simple. You blow Mike up, you blow bigger than you can ever be in one country. All CEO artists have the most money, and longer musical history." It was a hit out the park. Within a month of Mike's release, Dez was packed and moved to California. Flint set Dez up in a two-bedroom suite, on Sunset and Vine. With studio setup, they purchased beats from all over the world. M.A outta

Canada, S80 out New Orleans, Heartbeatz out of Atlanta, etc.

In eighteen months, Mike changed so much. He had loyal to my brother tatted around his neck, MIC on his right hand inside a gun, and AIM on his left hand inside a gun. It represented his stage name, which he went by in jail. The slim guy with the fade, was no more. He muscled up from eating and working out and had a haircut style like Nino on New Jack City. Even though he knew Flint was the boss, Flint had to give it to the growing kid, he had the image for the company. As long as he can deliver in the studio. He had Serenity already on standby, to contact every radio station, from the west coast to the south. To push interviews and get him involved in the hottest clubs on the market. Money talks, and they had enough to take a shot at the major leagues.

With the money saved for Mike, during his incarceration. He got a one-bedroom spot in Sunset and Vine, close to the label, in the same building as the studio. He understood the role of Dez, and he wanted to do the right things to make the money spent a success. The first night in the studio, Mike heard a banging beat from Heartbeatz, and before the beat started. He started talking grimy saying, "Head Targets was nothing to be fucked with. We got African hitters, we got money, and we are putting shit up if you try to stop it." Soon as the beat came on, a hard bass hit, and he said, "I'm Mic Aim, aim it right, when you shootin' aim it right."

Mic Aim – "Aim It Right" was instantly leaked on Youtube and Spotify. Vine clips was made after the same night recording the song. Dez shot a simple music video, of the fresh home street nigga. In jail slippers, sweats, and a wife beater. No jewelry, just a pocket full of money. It cut back and forth from him in a plushed suite studio, to him in the streets of LA, riding in a new white Beamer with a hand gun.

Flint thought this music industry shit was so fucking crazy, because Mike hadn't been in the streets 48 hours yet and had a million plays on a video clip. Not at the fact that the rapper was unknown, but the song was just recorded, and he haven't even got a car yet. Dez neither Mike, had a car yet, and the gun was for Serenity legally. This game was definitely whatever was shown, and whatever the audience bit on. It was enough to show Flint he was in the right business, and the fact Dez was a young talent, he knew about the right now demand. He knew everything about computers, software, etc. They had the right pieces to the puzzle. The very next day, Mic Aim had phone interviews lined up. With Carisma Cookie Jar, Hot 107.9, Power 95, Q93, Max 94.1, and 98.7. Everyone wanted to know where he came from, and how jail was.

NO CHANGE MORE PROBLEMS

Serenity set Mike up to do a Millions of Milkshakes event in LA. One night for promo and more artist exposure. Dez had them a car rented, since neither one of them had time to shop for one yet, with the growing fame. On a ride down Sunset, just passing Nickelodeon, they stopped to eat at a Roscoe's Chicken and Waffles.

While getting out the car on a side street, some young crip dudes, looking no more than the age of sixteen or seventeen. Started talking about cuz got on all that red, I wonder if he is banging or what. Mike being fresh home from jail, and on the same rules. Checked the biggest one in the group of five, and said, "I ain't no cuz, blood." Mike was piru, almost every young boy out New Orleans is blood. It's red city. The shortest boy with the young crips said, "Yo that's dude, with the Aim It Right video on the net." He started singing it, to make the dudes know what he was talking about. Dez didn't understand the fuss about blood or crip. He was excited about people noticing them in the streets so fast. He should've been more worried about what the big youngster was doing, as they were walking pass them, going into the restaurant.

With a call to their big homie, K-Do. The youngsters had a plan for the rapper, from disrespecting their color code. An embarrassing one after eating fried wings with waffles and syrup and drinking endless cups of sweet tea with lemonade. Dez and Mike left a twenty dollar tip and exited the other side. On cue, the biggest crip of the young five. Punched Mike with a round house, sending him to the ground. Dez tried to launch on the big fellow, but three other ones were quickly in on the action, kicking and beating him to the ground.

The short crip stood close by recording the whole thing saying, "Ladies and gentlemen, here we have Mic Aim, you know the slob that sings Aim It Right. Well right now he's getting' beatin' right. This is the consequences for disrespecting big home, K-Do. Where's your foreign whip nigga? Where's that rod you was holding in the video nigga?" The short crip was going on and on, then ended the video saying,

"Compton nigga." The youngsters broke out running into the dark night, disappearing blocks away. While on lookers where coming out the restaurant. Trying to help Mike and Dez, the only thing Mike was thinking about. Was his Nino haircut, not getting messed up. Mike only had a bust lip, because he tangled with the big youngster by himself. Dez got the worst of it really, because when he leaped in, three was on him. He had a black eye and a rib contusion. Good thing they still had their lives. Able to get to the rental, they made it out before police arrived.

Instead of going to the Millions of Milkshakes event, they were in route back to Sunset and Vine. The ride back, Mike was ranting about he need protection. He need his own whip and he need iron. This rap game is fraud. He can't be Mr. Nice guy, Mr. Changed to make this industry money. They will kill us out here, Dez we're walking targets. I'm from the hood, the 17th. Flint laying low. We out here on these public missions. I ain't no Hollywood nigga. Even though Dez ain't grow up like that, he understood that way of living. He didn't agree with the gang ties, but he agreed with them needing protection for this lifestyle.

Holding back the news from Flint, for as long as they could. Dez made the call back home to Ghana and told his family about the event that took place the night of the beatings. They knew the American way of living in a rap beef, would be blood spilled. Especially if one side had more wealth and power. They thought of Tupac and Biggie situation. This one was similar, but K-Do wasn't a rapper. They would later find out, K-Do was the underground weed connect. He had all the little crips moving packs, through LA and Hollywood. He fed them, opened up his home to them. He controlled their minds. Once fifteen years old and up, you could leave mommy and daddy house, and come sell drugs for K-Do. Everybody knew he had little kids riding metros, blue and red lines, and even riding bicycles with packs all over the city.

Dez's family decided to send one of their hitters, from Africa, to watch their son. Rhino, was a 6'6 250-pound, muscular black beast. If the opps see him, they'll retreat, or get in a far distance shootout. Because you couldn't fight this guy one on one, or three on one. It was a no win. The morning once Rhino arrived, Dez and Rhino drove to a Hollywood Hills mansion. To some rich South African white man, that his family had ties with. Dez rang the doorbell and said, "Black." That was the code word he was told to say upon his arrival. The man told him hold on, and what seemed like forever, was making Dez nervous. He waited it out, and the middle age white man brought a heavy guitar case, to the door. Dez said, "Thanks." The man said, "Courtesy of your father." Still not knowing the full connection between this man and his father. He was happy the transaction went just as planned. He nor Rhino touched the guitar case, until they were back to Sunset and Vine.

Mike was in the studio, going over some beats. When he saw Rhino, he smiled at the big guy, knowing he was on their team. When he saw the guitar case, he thought it was a big joke. He said, "Dez, you have Rhino, but what's with the guitar? Are ya'll tryna turn me into Prince or something? I'm a rapper, man, a rapper not a singer." In the middle of Mike's laugh, Dez popped opened the case, and all talks turned to whispers. Mike, "Oooh shit. Look at that machine." Rhino said, "It's a AK-47." Dez liked the glock nine, holding it up, checking the chamber and the clip out. Rhino pulled out the 40 and said, "This will be for you, Mike. I'll handle the machine." Rhino was forceful when it came to that murder shit. That was his resume. Good at killing shit. The perfect addition to the squad.

While Rhino searched thru the case for all the clips and ammunition, Dez and Mike recorded in the studio. Up until now, they haven't even told Flint about the event from nights ago. That would quickly change, when the young crips posted a video of them beating Mic Aim and his African CEO ass outside of a Roscoe's Chicken and Waffles. Everywhere videos, clips, and interviews were posted about the new rapper. The fight video was now also there.

Flint called Mike's phone, after watching the disturbing video. He told Mike put the phone on speaker, so Dez could hear. Flint said, "You know my current situation. You know I can't be everywhere with you all, that's why the label is setup like it is. But this is my company and Mike you're my brother, blood couldn't make us closer. I have an agreement with Dez's family, to make sure he's paid right and in good hands, but this video makes all three of us look bad. First of all, ya'll was supposed to be at a Millions of Milkshake event. Which we been working hard for, spending money to lift the label off the ground. Second of all, this shits gang related, and you know I don't fuck with gangs. That shits changed so much with the newer generation."

Flint was talking like he was older, but him and Mike was the same age. The next words that came out Flint's mouth, was what Mic was waiting on the whole time. "We gotta kill them niggas. It doesn't look good for you career wise, or home wise. Niggas in New Orleans not gone take Head Target serious, if outta town niggas steppin' on us. Without home behind us, we have nothing." Flint started screaming thru the speaker, "What was ya'lls plan? Did ya'll have one to fix this?" Before anyone could say anything, Flint disconnected.

Died Doin' Dirty Work: From the Dump

FLINT'S
AFRICAN
SURPRISE

Flint didn't know that Rhino was in Cali, until he got to the Sunset and Vine studio. Once spotting the big fellow, he knew Dez and Mike, already had been coming up with a plan. Dez gave him the run down on everything. Once Flint knew the whole story of what happened a night ago, up to Rhino's arrival, he wanted the problem stopped immediately.

Flint wanted Dez to search online for K-Do Twitter, Facebook, and Instagram, "You know wanna be niggas be flossing their shit, their where abouts, and all that." It ain't even take twenty minutes for Dez to find this pretty ass nigga on Twitter. On his header, he had; Youngsters Rule Blue Nation printed on a blue rag. That made Mike even madder. He was more angry about the colors, than his career to Flint. Mike started hollering to Dez saying, "Set his ass up. Send a bitch his way. He got long braids like a hoe. You know them hoes be on the nigga. He'll probably fuck anything that go his way." Dez had a better idea. "I'll set up a fake page with a bad bitch, and play on his top for a while, till he bites."

That same night, Dez had a phone number and address to the nigga in Compton. Flint had Serenity call off a prepaid phone, to seal the visit. Of course, she played her role. Anything Flint said, "The nigga talked like a bitch." They couldn't believe this nigga had that much control over these young boys. He knew money was a motherfucker; people would basically do anything for it. K-Do wanted to know what kinda car she was driving, and did she have friends. He also made it clear to not be on no funny shit, because it's his hood, and he had people everywhere. Mike and Dez knew these people he talked about, was probably the same group of youngsters that jumped them. They'll do anything for K-Do, so around the hood, they would definitely be strapped.

Dez went and switched the rental car out for a dark blue four door Ford F-250. When he got back, Mike switched the plates. Rhino started loading up. Flint had Serenity using two phones from the apartment. She would be on speaker with the guys in the truck. With the phone on mute, and she'll call K-Do from the other one, when they were close to the address. Flint grabbed the 380 and jumped in the truck. Dez, Mike, and Rhino said, "Naw big homie. We got this. You on the run. You need to be off the radar." Rhino said, "This really was his mission." "That's the reason he's in town," Dez said. Mike was about to say something, but Flint said, "I put this together. This is my name and reputation also. No telling how many little crip niggas is running around K-Do." Flint continued, "I wouldn't sleep right. If anything went wrong and I wasn't there. If I don't go, nobody goes, and that video stays up there and make us all look bad. To the industry and to our hometown."

With that said, Mike told Dez, "Start up the truck." Dez drove, Flint sat on the passenger side, and Rhino and Mike sat on the back seat. Once they got close to their location, they would let Rhino out. To climb in the back of the truck and lay flat with the AK-47. At ten o'clock p.m. when the mystery girl was supposed to be arriving, K-Do got a call saying she was just up the block. K-Do had a small three-bedroom home in the hood, surrounded by a short fence. His men were everywhere, standing in the road catching sells, sitting in the front yard smoking weed, sipping drank, and playing music.

Only two of the young boys were there at the time. The short one, was smoking with the older men, in the front yard. The big youngster, that went toe to toe with Mike, was in the back of the house clutchin' a Ruger 9. It was ten men total, including K-Do. Six of them was strapped. They had a .22, .38, Mac 11, 9 mm, .357, and a shotgun. They were always strapped, and today was no different. The only thing that would change on this day, would be the power.

Bare face and all, the men zoomed up the street, with the headlights off. Rhino on cue, raised up out the extended cab, and let off "TatTatTatTatTat." Shooting at niggas in the street, and the front yard. Smoke in the air, from bullets flying both ways. Didn't stop Flint and Mike, from hopping out the truck, and running to the beef. "Bok Bok" to the short crip that recorded the fight. "Record that, you short motherfucker," Mike screamed through a hail of bullets. Shorty was left onside the steps, where he was running inside, to warn K-Do. K-Do was caught slipping over a bitch. He didn't even have his rod on him during the shooting. Rhino and Flint ran up in the house, letting off rounds, incase more people was in there. If they were, they'll bust back or run scared. They were surprise, when they didn't see or hear nothing.

Outside, Dez hadn't left the truck yet. He was scoping out, with the glock in his hand. Once he seen Mike walking around the house by himself, he paid more attention to the guy hiding in a dark shed, behind the house. With a chrome piece, illuminating the night. Dez hopped out the driver side. With the keys, and slowly walked around the other side of the house. The big youngster had the drop on Mike. As Mike stepped out the light onside the house, into the dark backyard. The big youngster stepped out, and "Bok!" Dez stepped from behind him in the shed. The hunter became the hunted.

With a shot behind the head, the big youngster's lifeless body fell like a slinky. Bout time Dez and Mike got in the house, Rhino had found K-Do wrapped in a towel, like he just got out the shower. Flint said they searched each room, until Rhino found him. Flint heard Rhino telling K-Do, he should fuck him, take his manhood for fucking with Head Target. Flint heard the man cries and pleas. He told Rhino he had twenty large under the bed, and thirty pounds of good weed in the shed, in the trunk of the broke down 64. Rhino told the man, if the boss let you keep your life, we take the stuff then leave.

On cue, Flint walked in "BokBokBokBok". Rhino said, "Like I said, we take the stuff then leave." Mike carved "On Blood" into K-Do chest, to send a message to anyone who wanted to know how he handled the embarrassment, from the crips. Flint grabbed the twenty racks from the hole under the bed. Dez ran to start the truck and backed it to the shed. Rhino and Mike loaded the cab with the trees. They covered it with the car cover, off the 64. Then ran over two bodies laying in the road, before disappearing into the night. The total they knew they for sure murked that night, was five. They died doin' dirty work.

BACK DOWN SOUTH

With the money Flint had setup for Mike, the thirty pounds, and ten racks from the twenty taken from K-Do. He was heading back to New Orleans, with Dez and Rhino. Flint would use Agnes as a middle man again. Send him the kush, and him and Mike would meet up. Of course, Agnes would get his usual pay.

Before the Compton killings. Mike had plans to visit New York, Las Vegas, all around LA to perform, do interviews, and promote Head Target. Flint knew Mike could go back home for a while and get the heat off of them on the West Coast. The fact that K-Do sold drugs, and was a crip, anybody could've been responsible for his death. Especially with "On Blood" carved in his chest. Maybe the new Bompton, was responsible for it.

Mike, Dez, and Rhino rented a mansion in Eastover, and brought a black Tahoe, with dark tinted windows. Flint and Serenity stayed private in their Hollywood apartment, coming up with more plans. Dez set up a studio in Kenner, just right outside the city. The producers they had sending beats to Cali, was now able to come in person, and work from scratch. It was closer, everything felt right, it was how artist wanted to work. So, Mike had it all laid out for him. In the studio, promoting music, and fucking hoes was Mike's routine. Dez stayed close to his craft. Rhino was on point, doing his job watching out, and shopping for hot guns. He'll drive back and forth, from Eastover to Kenner, to run errands for Mike and Dez.

One evening, on Rhino's arrival back to the studio, he learned that some niggas that call themselves "One Life." Had visited a working Dez, trying to get studio time. Dez told them, what Mike told him to tell everyone who tried. "No, it was a private yo!" Dez told him, the dudes went on ranting about who the fuck we think we are, and we not even from around here. The main nigga, light skinned with dreads said, "They'll shut this bitch down, and no one will record." Leaving out the door, he heard them talking about robbing the equipment, and starting their own. That was enough for Rhino to get a security system installed.

They put cameras up every angle. Mike was trying to find out, who the fuck One Life was. He'll get them, before they get him. Dez described these dudes as best as he could. It was three of them, all tall with dreads, two of them were dark skinned. The leader was light skinned. He did the most talking, they just yes men to him, it's what it seemed like. He didn't see what they left in, but the last info, was the most reliable one to find them. They all had a "1" tatted on the left corner hairline, on their foreheads. Mike talked to people in the hood, he came up with, and searched online. No one ever heard of One Life. Maybe they were to new, to have a webpage. Meanwhile, Mike was preparing for a show at Ceaser's. For Q93 radio station, Saturday night.

All that Saturday evening, the radio station was pushing the show. Wild Wayne, was saying how he was so proud of a young fellow. Coming out the cities hostile environment, to getting the young people hyped up with his single, Aim It Right. Uptown Angela, got the ladies excited to come. By doing a personal interview with him. The hood was for sure going to be there, because they never saw him perform. Another guest would be there to see the rapper's first performance ever, and no one saw that coming. DJ Blaq N Mild, was running that beat all night.

The ladies were three, to everyone male. They had red bottoms, Jordans, pumps. The women were coming out their shoes, dancing, and shaking their ass. Smelling good of Selene and Nicki Minaj perfume. The men were fitted up in True and Robin jeans, dreads freshly twisted, sipping drinks, and grabbing all the ladies. A shadow in the club, over heard two youngsters talking about, "That's them niggas right there on stage. Mic Aim and his crew." One of them said, "Let's call Co." The other one said, "No, you know he is handling that lil biz we were on earlier today." "Yea, yea you right, we don't wanna interrupt that."

As it got closer to show time, the shadow stood behind them, to have an angle on them and the performance. The lights went out. Then the shadow seen one of the dread heads, draw a chrome piece from under his shirt. Before the lights came on, or Mike could get the first line of his song out. Nine shots echoed the club. His potna ran with the crowd. The shooter was poked up six times, in about three seconds, following the shots fired. Mike had no beef back home, but a hatin' nigga was always on the lose, trying to get stripes. On cue, Mike, Dez, and Rhino left out the side of the club. Where they had the Tahoe waiting.

Trying to figure out the events that just happened, they were all shook up. Mike kept saying, "That's them One Life niggas." One thing about niggas in the city, if they say they gone do something, they gone do it. Niggas gotta die now. Even if we gotta hit the wrong niggas, to find them niggas, somebody gone feel it. Rhino told him, on their way exiting, he seen a gunman laying slump. With the piece still in hand. They had a couple bodies shook from getting ran over in the stampede, but as far as dead, he looked like the only one. Dez said, "Maybe security or an undercover shot him." Rhino said, "He knew how bullets sound, and every bullet that ranged threw the club that night, was from one gun." All three of them rode back to Eastover in silence, wondering how the gunman got hit. He died doin' dirty work.

The shadow had a cab waiting for him, on Frank Street. He calmly walked up and said, "Eastover." He made it there, before the owners of the home. When the black Tahoe pulled up, they questioned the lights being left on. Rhino pulled out the 40 he had on him and took the 9 Dez was holding. Mike and Dez waited, while Rhino checked out the crib. He walked in the living room, to find a fresh to death Flint. Sitting on the couch, smokin' a blunt, watching the news. Rhino knew Flint was the only one, who knew where the spare key was, to their rented mansion. He also had a good guess, that Flint knew what happened to the gunman in the club. Mike and Dez was both surprise, and happy to see Flint. They knew it was too risky for him to move like them, because he was a wanted man. Flint told them he couldn't miss Mike's first time performing, especially in their hometown. Even though no one seen

Mike perform, they still saw the crowd was there for him. It was a packed house.

Flint told them how he caught a flight there that evening and paid a cab driver to roll him around the city. He stopped by the studio and checked out the crib. Then headed to Ceaser's for the concert. He told them about the two niggas he saw, plotting up something on the dance floor. He mentioned them calling someone, named Co. Mike jumped off the couch and said, "Yo Dez, didn't you mention one of the three dudes, from that studio visit, being referred to as Co?" Dez said, "Yea, that must be the leader. The light skinned one with the dreads." Flint knew he couldn't leave back out, until they dead them niggas. After learning they had visited the studio. No telling how much more they knew. The four of them watched the news clips and passed the blunt. No one could see who killed the gunman.

ONE LIFE CO

The next morning, they headed out to the studio, Flint wanted to check out things. He felt like he been out the loop, since he been staying in Cali. They left one beef in Cali, only to run into another back home. While their minds were still on the events, that happened last night. They found smiles and small talk, about how their success had been. Dez was about to put the key in. Mike was bragging to Flint, on how his new music was sounding, and saying all that beef shit got us hotter. Everybody checking for a nigga now, seeing what's next. Flint said, "It's also making them a target. Everywhere they look, somebody new got a problem." Mike said, "It comes with the game. You wanted it." Dez screamed out loud, "What the fuck?"

The door had been kicked in. When Dez was putting the key in, the door just opened up. He had forgotten to put the alarm on, because they were rushing, putting the show disc together for the concert. The guys rushed in to find the hard drive, the keyboard, the speakers, the screens, the mic, and pounds gone. While two of the members, of One Life, was staking out the concert. Co was Easter egg hunting in the studio. The only thing left behind, was camera footage. They wouldn't report it. They'll study the tape carefully and take action. Flint setup a meeting with Officer Agnes, to meet with Dez. Dez was to give Agnes the tape and all info he knew on One Life.

Officer Agnes called Flint an hour later, with Earth shattering news. The dude they call "One Life Co", real name is Coren Minter. The same Coren Minter, that was Mike's celly at St. Landon. Flint and Agnes said at the same time. Agnes gave Flint all info listed for Co. His girlfriend, new born baby, and mom lived in a small apartment in Kenner city. Flint would run it all down to Mike and see exactly how he wanted to handle it. Mike replied just how Flint expected, "He had his niggas try to murk me. We kill everything he love, then we will eventually get him." Flint was with everything, except for killing the baby. He thought bout how him and Serenity had been trying to make a baby, and how special that was. He gave the mission to Mike and Rhino and stayed out of that one.

Dez rented an Impala, Mike changed the plate, and Rhino loaded up for the creep. One Life Co had been bold. He had robbed a studio bare face and had reckless youngsters as shooters on his team. Co didn't know Mike was on the other side. Of any of the events that had taken place. Matter of fact, Co didn't even order his men, to shoot at the club that night. They were supposed to follow the owner of the studio, to make sure the studio would be a go. They just ended up at the Mic Aim concert, and the live wire dread head committed an act, he can no longer take back.

Co didn't listen to the radio, to know his old celly was even in town, and had a concert. He would never have turned on Mike. He didn't learn the beef was with Mike, until watching the news. The night of the shooting, after he broke in their studio and robbed him. The goon that ran after the shots were fired, tried to explain to Co, that he tried to stop the live wire from opening fire. But he was determined to get a body and ended up getting bodied. Co told the scary goon, that they fucked up bad. He told him, that the dudes they're now beefing with, were for real with the shits. He explained how him, and Mic Aim met. He explained the whole flooding St. Landon, how Flint took care of him, like he was one of them. He told the young goon, their eating right now because of them. All the money put on his books, were from them. He came home with a few racks, from jail.

Co had his young hitter watch the apartment complex, immediately. He told him if he seen anything suspicious, contact him. He would be tryna find Mike and make it right, but in his head, he knew that wouldn't happen. It had definitely went to far already. Bullets flown.

The first night watching the apartment, the young goon noticed a gray Impala. With a darked skinned man driving, block in and out the complex. He fell asleep in the car that night. To wake up in the morning, to find the same car parked in a spot, in front the apartment Co and his family lived in.

While the young goon slept, he didn't know he was being watched. Rhino not only sniffed out Co lookout man. He also seen what time his mother went to her hotel job. About 6 a.m. that morning, dressed as a maid, Co's mother entered a white Neon and headed to work. With his girlfriend just having a baby, she would be resting. He put the call into Mike, explained it to him, and told him tomorrow morning would be a go. While passing the lookout car, seeing a waking up young goon. Co's young hitter, called him and told him about the suspicious car, and guy. Co told him, if he seen it again, call him and he'll head there and get the business clear.

The next morning, Rhino and Mike was on point. Two silencers, rope, and tape were what they needed for this mission. The same schedule Rhino was on the day before, when Co lookout man was asleep, and his mom was heading to work. He repeated. There the lookout man was sleep in the car. At 5:50 a.m. Rhino and Mike exited the rental, and caught the mom walking away from locking the door. Bare face, they didn't plan on leaving any witnesses. Rhino shoved the silencer in her back and forced her to unlock the door. The woman pleaded saying, "If it's money ya'll want, I have none." She said, she was just a hard working woman, and she had a new born grandbaby inside. Rhino told her, "Shut up. Get in there and thank her son for the blood that was upon them."

Once inside, they had one mission, kill and get out. Mike tied up the mother's arms and ankles. Rhino chased the running girlfriend, grabbed her and said, "Any loudness I shoot the baby." Rhino closed the room door, tied up the girl's arms and ankles, pulled out his big African dick. Then shoved it up the not healed womb. Her cries were heard through the door. Mike didn't know what the fuck Rhino was thinking. They were supposed to kill and get out. Rhino was so deep in her. He had her blood, sweat, and tears on his dick. He put a piece of tape on her mouth, pulled out. Put some spit on her asshole, then forced inside. Her muffled screams came through the tape. The whole time, the baby was in the room crying. He only stopped when he heard Mike banging on the room door, saying someone was knocking, next plan.

Rhino used her gown, wiped his dick off. Grabbed his gun and told her shut that baby up or he will. He left the tied up girlfriend bleeding and closed the room door. They discovered Co's young goon outside the door. Rhino untied the mom and told her let him inside. The young goon was walking through the door, saying Co was on his way, to checkout a car that's been hanging around. When "BINK!" the hammer sent him face first into the glass table. Rhino told him call Co off. The young goon told Co everything was fine, that he was in the apartment, moms was late for work, and the car was just a rental. For someone who lived in the apartment complex. Once he hung up, Mike whispered a silenced shot to the back of his head.

He died doin' dirty work.

HAMMS
ROBBERY

Flint was laying in a W Hotel suite, on Facetime. While Reba and her homegirl, Karen, scoped out the next take. Hamms Food and Money Center. Ever since the beef with One Life Co, money was low. They needed to recoup the loss of the recordings, and being that Flint left Serenity in Cali, money was being spent keeping up with bills and promo. So, no incoming money was coming in at the moment. When Hurricane Katrina hit, a lot of the girls from the projects, that left the city. Got groceries, received money, and sent money from Hamms.

While their men, was further outta state hustling, and hitting licks. The women stayed close with the kids. Reba put Mike on it, because she knew the bind they were in. He been fucking her for years, so she's always down for Mike. Her friend, Karen, came in on the take. Just to assist Reba, and she needed some extra cash, to support her coke habit. Flint did a google search on the whole area and had Dez rent a Malibu. Mike and Rhino purchased two can-am 4-wheelers, and because it was an hour away, they used Karen gated home.

After drying four spray painted masks, four different colors, and getting the number of employees. Time the owner move money out the store, and all camera angles. Flint put it in motion.

At seven o'clock p.m. the next night, Flint and Dez was sitting in front of Hamms, with Mike and Rhino behind the store spraying the cameras. All they had to do was locate the most money, and have it back in the city, within the next two hours. On cue, Dez walked in the money center and distracted the young girl behind the glass, looking no more than eighteen years old. He told her he was trying to send some money out the country. When two masked gunmen walked right next to them, in the same building, only split by a door. Putting everybody on the floor, and cashiers opening registers. They hit five registers, when Dez seen the young girl opening a safe behind the glass. She was trying to make a run for it, out the back door exit. Dez put a quick call to a outside waiting Flint.

Smooth as a cat, Flint crept around the store, mask behind his head. Banger in hand. Spotted the young girl, slid the mask on. She tried to tase. Bok! Slumped her, took the bag, then jumped on a waiting 4-wheeler. Mike and Rhino fled to the 4-wheelers, with bags full from the registers. Flint rode with Mike. The three disappeared on back roads, all the way to Karen's. After panicking, like a customer, after a robbery. Dez hopped in the rental, and checked out the scenery, before heading to Karen's.

In the two car garage, at Karen's house. Waited Mike's black Tahoe, two 4-wheelers, and a rental Malibu. After changing, the guys took the Tahoe. The girls took the rental, with all the money. Just in case anything happened, along the drive back. Safe in the city, back downtown at the W Hotel. The girls counted up the money, while the fellas enjoyed their rush from the take. It was like taking candy from a baby. Each bag from the registers, had two thousand. With a total of ten thousand dollars. The safe bag the girl carried, had fifty thousand dollars. Flint gave the girls five thousand and made sure he got familiar with Karen, incase he needed her down the line.

Karen was feeling Flint, because when the guys was heading out, to stash the money in Eastover. She told Reba, she was staying, and probably getting a room at the W. That night, she opened up to Flint about her life. How she always was on her own, and messed with older guys, to eat and pay her bills. She was single, no kids, just addicted to coke, and the fast life. Flint heard enough from her. To know he'll never be with her, fall for her, or be intimate. Even though he knew he would never leave Serenity, he sometimes questioned how strong he could be. To hold back the urges of fucking other women, that threw themselves at him. He knew one thing that night for sure. Karen could make him a lot of money.

F-GIRLS

Flint sent a long text message to Mike, about their next hustle. With Flint explaining it in full to him. The only thing left, was for Mike to seal it up with Reba. Mike cared for Reba, but not relationship wise. So that night, Mike fucked her good. While talking to her, legs in the air, putting pressure on that fat cat. She tried to go against the offer, but he was forceful. He told her, if she loves him, she'll make this a success. Her friend was already in, and he wouldn't look at her any different. Matter of fact, Mike said he'll be closer now. She'll see him more, and that was enough to bring Reba in on the plan.

Reba and Karen would be the first Fuck Girls, for short, F-Girls. Flint learned a lot of game in Cali, while Mike was serving time. With a rental car switched ever week or two, Mike coming on and off the road. Dez and Rhino fixing the studio back up, and the F-Girls with whatever to make paper. Nothing could stop this new hustle.

Flint started them off slow and local, to see how things work with them. They'll head out to cities such as; Lafayette,

Monroe, Kenner, and downtown New Orleans. They'll get two rooms away from each other. Flint would post up in one, and the girls would be in the other. Flint made sure they had everything to be presentable. They had fly pictures that showed off their bodies, the prepaid cards were loaded for whatever. Back page, quick net purchases, travel, etc. They were charging tricks anywhere from one hundred and fifty quickies, to five hundred dollars for a couple of hours.

The money was no problem, but the cops were. They had to ask the clients "were they involved with law enforcement, trying to entrap them?" like three times. On the first call, when they pulled up to the address, and while they were coming up to the room. Sometimes the cops would come to the room anyway, but as long as the girls didn't offer any kind of sexual advances, the cops couldn't arrest them.

After making a lot of money in the local areas, it was time to hit other cities and states. Birmingham, Montgomery, Nashville,

Atlanta, Houston, and Tampa. Houston was a lucrative spot but was also a close call. Staying on the southwest side, Flint had a suite at the extended stay of America. The F-Girls were staying at the La Quinta. Mike flew in Bush airport, to do some promo work, and to spend a little time with Reba. The things he had to do from time to time, to keep her going. Flint let Mike and Reba stay in the suite. While Flint and Karen kept the money going, at the La Quinta. Whenever Karen got a trick, Flint would sit in the rental and checkout the parking lot.

One of Karen's clients looked very familiar to Flint, from the parking lot. Light skinned with dreads, and when he turned his head before entering the hotel, Flint saw the "1" on his forehead. Man, this can't be One Life Co. Before Flint reacted, he made a call to Mike. Mike answered, while getting head from Reba. He pushed her out the way, when he heard the news. Flint grabbed his strap, tucked it, and slid key on the side door. To get to the room quicker. Once to the room door, he listened, but couldn't hear anything. He stuck the key in and thank God everything happened so fast. No one put the inside latch on the door. It turned green, and he drew down on a nigga on top of Karen, dick inside her. Knife to her throat, asking a lot of questions. Once the man heard the person coming in the room, he jumped out the pussy. On cue, with his gun turned toward Flint, four shots echoed. Sending what was definitely Co, over the bed. Karen grabbed everything of hers, before her and Flint, calmly walked down the stairs to the car. They picked up Mike and Reba and got the fuck outta Texas.

On the ride back to New Orleans, Karen was shook up. Telling them everything that happened in the room, before Flint saved her. They all learned that Rhino did some sick shit, in that family hit. They killed everybody in the apartment, except the new born. After killing the mom, Co's girlfriend, and his goon, Rhino threw the baby out the window. The baby didn't die from the second floor drop. But he's been in bad condition ever since. Inside bleeding, broken bones, and face surgery.

Co knew Mike would be in town for Houston Promo. He also knew Reba was on back page. She was supposed to be the girl in the room, but Mike and Reba stayed at the suite. Co was a broken man. He had a death sentence for Mike, and whoever was involved, or around him. With Co left behind hit four times, Flint and Mike could shake the girls back. To forgetting about that shit and getting back to the money. What no one noticed in the car, was that Karen was calm to fast and easy. Almost like nothing happened, just earlier. She now felt loved. No man had ever protected her. They all fucked, gave her money, and went their way. Here was a good looking street nigga, being there for her. Killing a nigga, that was taking advantage of her, and she ain't never fucked him. That made Karen want Flint even more, but she knew he wouldn't go for it. He had Serenity, and this was just business.

Making it back to New Orleans, they took off for the day. Mike and Reba went to the Eastover pad, while Flint and Karen, checked in the W Hotel downtown. Karen ran some bath water for Flint and ordered food. She presented him with a Rolex watch, she took from one of her clients. Flint couldn't believe she gave him such an expensive gift, and he wasn't her man. He thanked her by letting her suck his dick and balls, until he came in her throat. Karen had a plan, and it was working. She wanted Flint.

Died Doin' Dirty Work: From the Dump

SURPRISE SERENITY

The whole while the events down south were happening, Serenity had an inside ear. Reba kept it street with Serenity. They had been knowing each other a very long time. They had been messing with Flint and Mike for years. Serenity put out a few dollars to Reba, just to keep an eye on her man. She told her about the Hamms robbery, and the newly found F-Girls.

Serenity wasn't to surprise, to the fact they were getting money. He went back down south, to make a few more things happen. She put the phone on mute, and lost her fucking mind, when she found out about girls being around her man. Reba told her the truth, or at least all that she really knew. Her and Karen worked, the guys just secured them, and handled expenses on the road. Reba and Mike still had their fuck relationship, with benefits.

Flint was loyal to Serenity, and that was that. Serenity ain't wanna hear nothing, after hearing the female name. "Karen, Karen, Karen, securing them, and handling expenses" Serenity screamed "what about my security with this fucking baby." Her and Reba froze up, for what seemed like minutes. No one knew about a baby, Flint haven't even heard the news yet. Serenity begged Reba not to mention anything, until she had words with Flint. Serenity hung up and cried, trying to figure it out. Mike heard the news, listening through the door of the room.

Mike busted through the door, to a worried Reba. Already knowing what was up, He wanted her to just speak on everything. She tried to beat around the bush, she said, "It was a homegirl. Just going through some problems," and she was being of help to her. Mike grabbed her phone and went to the last call. Now Ima ask one more time, "what the fuck is going on?" Reba shouted, "She's pregnant. Okay. She's pregnant. I told her everything, she was worried about Flint being back here, while on the run. She knows about the money and the F-Girls. She's upset, but she loves Flint. She knows he loves her and won't do anything to hurt her."

Mike had to tell Flint the exciting news, he was having a baby Myers. He didn't know how he would take the news, about Serenity knowing everything going on, but he was his brother. He had to be straight up and real about everything. Reba's careless acts was the start of all this. Bout time Mike got to Flint suite, he was already on the phone with Serenity. Karen was laying in bed silent, Mike was standing up by the muted TV, and Flint was pacing back and forth. Going back and forth, with a screaming Serenity. All they heard in the background, was screaming.

Once Flint got off the phone, he told Mike get Reba in line, before he has to. He also said we got work to do. It's a new addition to the family. More money. Karen was jealous. That's the only way to put it. Just before Mike got there, and the phone call from his little pregnant trophy. She was getting fucked like a main chick, by the freshly shaved head street nigga with the thick dick. Now, it's back to work.

Once Mike left, Karen asked Flint was their little fling over with. He coldly said, "we have nothing, this is business. We crossed the line with having sex." Flint told Karen from the beginning, he had Serenity. He loves Serenity. Now more feelings were involved. He had to admit. Karen was off the coke, she had thickened up, from eating good and getting fucked. The 5'8 dark stallion, with legs like a track star, could be a man's dream girl. If he didn't know about her prostitution, life, and drug habit. She had her own crib, car, and no kids. Flint knew the truth, so she was considered strictly business. He never touched her until recently, when she sucked his dick.

With an attached F-Girl, and a pregnant lover, Flint had major problems brewing. The only thing he could do, is make enough money out his newly found system, before things blew up in his face. Mike would be in charge of the girls, on the next run. Flint figured tension would be down, if he stayed put, while the girls worked. He could take the time to meet up with Serenity, make things right, and celebrate the baby news. Serenity had plans of her own, and if Flint didn't bring a hose pipe, the fire would spread.

HE'S NOT DEAD

Mike and the girls made a stop, right off the coast of Florida, to a Motel 6. Mike did things a little different from Flint. When he got to a spot, he got his room next to the girls. It's good for security purposes, but bad for police busts. Someone must have followed them to the coast, because the escape route he used, was planned for a close hit to home.

Reba in call, came right at dark. He asked how much it would cost for four hours. He admired her body, and he was in town on family vacation. A stack up front, everything seemed legit. She sent Karen in the room with Mike and got ready for her client. Once he got there, Mike examined him from the next room. He looked like every other trick. In a hurry to get some ass, spend some cash, and strike out. Multiple hours were usual. Every few cities the girls get to, some ballers would flash their money, saying they can spend whatever. How much for the night?

The guy was light skinned. But had a skull cap on, a hoodie, and sweats. It was cool out by the waters, so that was regular.

While in the room, the guy was getting sucked up, but wasn't taking off no clothes. Reba found that strange, but was doing her job, to bring daddy that money. While hitting her from the back, she felt something hard slapping against her, that wasn't a dick. Without making it obvious, she told him to go get some lube out the bathroom, she wanted it in her ass. He decided he would go get that and reveal himself with the gun. Kill her, and whoever else get in his biz. It was One Life Co. In the two minutes it took Co to get the lube, Reba had placed a text to Mike. TROUBLE.

Co returned to a scrambling Reba, putting on clothes, with phone in hand. Skully off, clearly seeing the "1" tattoo, dread head man. His eye's showed death. Speaking no words, he pulled out the black bitch, and "Bok!" Sent Reba flying to the floor. Mike slid the key in on cue with the gun sound, "Bok! Bok! Bok!" He sent three more to the door. Then broke out running through the door. With a backed up Mike, ducking from bullet shots. Co had enough time to jump the second floor railings, on to the front hood of his waiting car.

Mike returned fire on him, but Co was moving like a man possessed. "Bink! Bink! Sccssh! Sccssh!" The body of the car being hit, and glass shattering. Nonstop, Co hit the highway west, going back towards New Orleans. All Mike could holler, while driving Reba to the hospital was, "Fuck! Fuck! He's not dead! That motherfucker is not dead!" Flint shot that nigga four times, "Karen hollered. She witnessed the nigga fly over the bed, not moving. Mike dropped the two of them off at the hospital, and they were to fly back after Reba healed up. Mike headed back. Co is still alive.

EVERYONE ON GUARD

With Co on the loose seeking revenge, Reba recovering from a bullet to the stomach. Serenity wanting to kill Karen, and Flint still on the run. Everyone was on guard, and even worst, everyone was located in the small city of New Orleans. Before the F-Girls could work again, Flint wanted the beef dead. He felt like his camp was at risk, and too open with the prostitution deal. Not only did they need to kill Co, they needed money. They were comfortable with the money from the takes and the sells but feeding a whole team and family. It would not last.

Leaving everybody staying at the Eastover mansion, Flint and Serenity got a suite at the Loews Hotel downtown. They were still at it about the F-Girls, his position in that, and not fully trusting him or them hoes. The only thing she did trust, was her next plans. They were to make enough money, to hope Flint would leave the F-Girls alone for good. Either by that, or by killing her target.

When Serenity was working for Humana, doing school online. She had a lot of connects. Some people through her company, worked for Pharmacy distributors all throughout Louisiana. It was a small group, that could get certain drugs, when no one else could. They got all kinds of discounts. The sweet thing about this was, pharmacies would call the distributors for re-ups. They drove their own trucks, with a trailer, unmarked. They delivered like paper boys, five days a week. The same routes.

Flint had Dez check out a specific location. In the Baton Rouge area, on airline. They have a Walgreens and CVS at a red light, only split by a street. Flint wanted to know exactly how long they would have, how many cops he seen in the area, etc. Serenity told him, the truck stops at most pharmacies, that's independent. CVS, Walgreens, and a lot of mom and pop places. Just like she said, at eleven o'clock a.m. the truck was at the first stop, CVS.

Within minutes tops, he was putting the dolly back in, and heading over to Walgreens. Where he repeated the same mission. It was a lot of traffic around, and customers in and out, but only two cops passed the main highway. None passed the street by the stores, not one time. This was going to be easier than a bank.

The next morning, the hungry men piled in a rented GMC truck. With a boat cutter, four painted masks, and regular clothes. They wouldn't need weapons, because burglary of a pharmacy only carries ten years, and that's not aggravated. They pulled in. Once the truck pulled in. The guys watched the middle aged white man load up the dolly, lock back up, then walk the dolly in the front door. Rhino hopped out, popped the lock, and slide the door/ramp down. Dez backed the truck up to the trailer. Rhino, Mike, and Flint through every crate full of drugs into the truck. Bout time the man came back with the dolly, the guys was on the side street, heading to the storage unit. Since it was broad day, they dropped the inventory off. Switched cars and headed back to New Orleans until the heat went down.

ICU

After making forty large, off the pharmacy truck lick, the team had other plans. You would think everyone would be on some lay low shit, but the truth was, a mad man was still on the loose. Somewhere close, looking for blood. Karen was doing research, while looking after Reba. She had found out that Co only child, was at the Children's Hospital, still fighting for his life. That was the news Flint needed to hear. They knew the kid was fucked up, but they never pursued it, because it was a child. Flint didn't want anything to do with it in the first place, but now that Co was making their life that much difficult, he wanted them both dead. The order was to kill Co and Jr.

After a lot of going back and forth, with who was going to be responsible for this hit. The crew suggested, Serenity, was perfect for it. Not only did she agree, but she also felt like she needed to show her man her worth. Flint didn't want her involved with nothing, that's the reason why she was left back in Cali, in the first place. Now with her being pregnant, Flint felt he had to protect her even more. Everyone in the crew knew they'll be at risk.

Co knew everyone, except Serenity. She wasn't around for any of the in counters, with Co or One Life. She now had to play nurse. She had to get in Co's business. She had to find the perfect way to kill them and get them out of their lives.

With a worried call to the hospital, Serenity manipulated her way into room 215. Around 6 p.m. Coren Minter was sitting beside his son. Holding his scarred hands, telling him how much he loved him, and how sorry he was. Even though the baby was small, he still knew he could hear him, and understand him. It had been some time passed since the incident, and he was there each day, holding on to the last item left in his world. The only time Co wasn't there with Jr. Was when he was out trying to kill Mike and his team. He'll always update Jr. with the missions. That evening, he was telling him, "I'm trying son. I keep busting at them. I'm on their trail. I won't stop until their dead."

As he was showing pictures of the people involved to his son, a nurse walked in. To check the baby's wounds, feed him, and give him his regular routine meds. Co was speechless, as he seen the new nurse. Trying to overlook her beauty, he was on guard as always. He asked her name, and said he never seen her there before. It was the same nurses and doctors that cared for his son. The nurse stopped what she was doing, seductively walked towards Co. Who sweared she looked like GiGi, with hips like Amber Rose, pointed to her perky breast. Where the name tag sat, and said, "My name is Angela. The kids call me Ms. Seals. You, sir, can call me whichever you like", in heavy accent like Rihanna. She told him she usually works the whole hospital, has her own office, and usually be gone around four o'clock p.m. This was not her normal job, but since staff was short, she filled in a few hours for ICU. She knew he was buying everything she said, because he relaxed. Co was quite handsome to her, she just knew the reason she was there. The only reason was for blood. She convinced Co, that the regular nurses would be back soon.

In the meantime, they chatted about his son, the condition he was in, and what was next for his release. Co didn't have anything planned. He told her the story about what happened to his family. Even though she knew more details than him, she knew the next sympathy play would work perfectly. "Mr. Coren Minter, here's my number. I'm starting my own home health care. I was inspired to do this, by people like little Jr. here. I will be affordable since I'm just starting out, and since you don't have a lady to do certain things around the house, you may have one here." She pointed at her curves, turned towards Jr., kissed him on the forehead. Then through her butt left to right, while walking out the door.

Co made a mental note, to check the roster for a Ms. Seals, and to call her soon as little man was released. He could've used someone at the house. Since relocating, it's been awhile since he had a women's touch. She could watch Jr. while he hunts.

Died Doin' Dirty Work: From the Dump

HIS GIRL, HIS GIRL

Pulling up to the tall black gates, Serenity, known as Ms. Seals. Punched in #0100. Once inside, she seen how Co was really living. He told her on the phone, he stayed in Manhattan Palace. She had passed there a million times in her life, but never had reason to enter. She knew it was for people with money, but never imagined that amount of money. Those condos must have ranged from two hundred thousand to $1.5 million easy. Co must have had a damn good job, or a damn good job had him.

Serenity giggled to herself at the reason he'd allowed her to see where he lived. Because she checked out right on the roster search. There was a Ms. Seals that worked at the hospital. They agreed to a twelve month in home health care contract. Her salary would be two hundred and fifty dollars a week, paid meals, and gas. Not too bad for her first gig at this. Pulling up to the three story brick condo, that looked every bit like a mansion. She noticed her little used Honda, didn't fit in the neighborhood of latest model cars.

Even Co had a blacked out Range parked in front the door. He opened the door, embraced her with a big hug, and told her to make herself comfortable. She was more comfortable dressed this time, instead of the scrubs Co saw her in at the hospital. She had on black tights and a fitted white shirt, showing her breast nipples. She asked how was Jr. doing, and he decided to take her on a tour of the lavish pad, before getting to her duties.

The first floor was dark, almost like a cave. Big kitchen, with a back door that leads to the courtyard. The furniture was black leather, it was definitely for a man. The second level was all white. That's probably how Yo Gotti crib is, she thought to herself. It looked like no one ever visits that area. The third story was lime green, like Seattle Seahawks loud color. It was where Jr. slept. He stayed in the bright room, to hide his scarred body. As he was getting older, he started noticing his problems, and other kids problems were different. He would never have a normal child hood. Co knew this, and that was the main reason to hire Ms. Seals.

Being that they walked up the stairs, she didn't notice the elevator that set off to the opposite side.

Jr's wounds and bones were pretty much healed, but his heart and scars were not. Even though her whole reason for being there, was to end them, her heart went out to Jr. He was just a child, and even though Serenity was pregnant, and not showing yet. She thought about her baby. Wondering what she was having and couldn't imagine someone being this close to ending her seed, or her lover's life. She snapped out of it and smiled at the little boy. She asked what was his favorite food. She would order pizza, bathe him, and clean his room. Her routine all that week was simple; washing laundry and cleaning, cooking and ordering food, playing games with Jr., and giving him his meds.

She stayed downtown at the Loews. Money was not an issue, she still had the Cali crib and Beamer. She only had turnt down for her mission. While at work, she'll text Flint always updating him. After work they'll end their night together. The only thing different, was the amount of time they were apart. She had been through Flint being in jail, on the run, leaving her in Cali. While running around with the F-Girls, to now being around his enemy, more than him. It was a lot of times Co would leave her and Jr. there early in the day, then call and ask could she stay. Serenity swore, that was the nights he hunted for the people, involved with his family hit. He never mentioned revenge, or the names of anyone to her. Even he told her, his money came from a deceased family member. He was full of secrets, but she knew the most important ones.

One night Co came home, to a sleeping Ms. Seals on the couch. Jr. was asleep up stairs in his room. Co cut off the TV, and the rest of the lights, then set onside her while she slept. He admired her beauty and stroked her face. She snuggled up to him. Co embraced it and you would think that Flint's girl, was now his girl.

BOWTIE

"What's taking so long Serenity? You've been on this mission for too long. I didn't want you involved in the first place." Flint began questioning. Serenity was feeling soft these days with the baby growing inside of her, and the close relationship she had built with Jr. Flint didn't know about the encounter between her and Co. Even though nothing escaladed from the snuggle up on the couch. She knew Co was the enemy, so it could be no excuse. "What about the bitch, Flint? What about that bitch, Karen? Have you taken care of that yet?" Serenity also felt like she had been around too long also. They both had guilt, but they were one. They wouldn't let no one get between them.

Flint held his head down and told Serenity, "I love you more than anything in this world. If getting her out the picture will ease your mind more during this process. Then that's what it will be." Serenity had Flint's phone behind her back with Karen's number dialed. While in convo about Karen was discussed. Serenity had wanted her to hear it out of his mouth that the F-Girls would not exist much longer. Just as Serenity started kissing him, she hung up. She told Flint, "In the morning, I will go through with my mission.

Early that morning Serenity noticed a smoke gray Durango in the spot Co usually parks in. She didn't think nothing of it since he had a little money. He could have bought a new whip, or it could've been a rental. Once she got in the front door, she was welcomed by a tall dark skinned Muslim. Who was wearing a black blazer, white button up, blue jeans, Doc Martins, and a colorful bowtie.

Once he stepped in the light, she could see his fresh shaved head. He told her to have a seat, but she reached in her purse instead. He pulled out a .357 from behind his back and insisted, "Serenity have a seat." All she could think was, "How does he know my name? And who the fuck is this guy?"

After Serenity had a seat, he proceeded to say that he was a friend of One Life Co. Co had suspicion of who she really was. Even though Serenity had never blown her cover, Co was never at peace with his life, so he hired a hitman to look into Ms. Seals life. See her connections to all of this. "All of a sudden, you just fell out of the sky to look after Jr., Bowtie is the name by the way."

Serenity knew she was in a lot of trouble but stayed calm. He told her that he had been following her to and from work. And even though he had never seen anything fishy, the tip they got from Karen last night, sealed the deal.

Karen had been spending time with Flint, while Serenity was out on the mission. She knew what she had with Flint was slowly coming to an end, because of Serenity and the baby. She was securing herself, by getting all the information Serenity would leave for Flint, on Co for herself. She had the address, gate code, phone number, etc. So, when he got the call from Karen, he knew the play, and quickly turned the table. All she wanted, was for them to kill Serenity, and the baby inside of her. Karen thought if Serenity could be out the way, she'll have Flint for herself.

As Serenity shook her head in disbelief, she asked, "So what will ya'll do with me?" On cue, a helicopter was coming down above the condos, and landed in the middle of the courtyard. He told her, she will be joining Co and Jr., but first he needed her phone to contact Rhino. He had a special request from Co, to kill him in a death fight, and being that Serenity was held captive. It would be easy to lure him in. With a call to Rhino explaining the details, he knew what to do. Head to the courtyard. No weapons, no team. If he contacts Flint, Serenity dies. If he tries anything other than what told, Serenity dies. Co, Jr., and the pilot waited in the chopper.

Died Doin' Dirty Work: From the Dump

FIGHT OUT, FLIGHT OUT

Not telling the crew a thing, Rhino pushed it from the East to the Westbank. Mind racing, wondering why this clown wanted to fight him, and not be on no murder shit. Meanwhile, Bowtie had done went through Serenity's things. Found a small handgun, and a dose of propanol. While walking behind her, through the back door to the helicopter. He shot her up with the needle, and she went limp in seconds. He carried her to the chopper. Signaled them off and waited for Rhino arrival.

Pulling up to the address giving, Rhino had to look for red lights coming out of a courtyard. Once he spotted the lights, he noticed the gate had an opening in it. Loud music blasted from the surround sound, all over the crib and outside through the courtyard. A loud voice came over the speakers of the now paused music, "Welcome my stupid friend. See, you are about ten minutes too late. Serenity has left the building. As I' am speaking to you now, she should be crossing over the ocean with her new family. You, my friend, are left here to die and your rapper friends should mourn the same way Co did over his family." Bowtie let out a scream, then locked the gate.

Rhino never seen the first lick coming. Boom! To the right side of the head, with a balled up chain. Swollen, and leaking blood from by his temple. He took some big slow hard swings hitting air, as he tried to regain his footing. Bowtie then tased him, like a dirty cop would do. His strong frame would not go down. It seemed like he was more machine or animal, than human. Rhino hollered out through shaky lips, "Give me a fair shot. I came here just as you told me to. Without weapons, my team, or no surprises to your fight out. May the best man win." Stopping the taser for a brief moment, Bowtie responded, "See nothing in this life is fair. I' am Muslim, and everybody in this country is against me." Rhino shouted, "I' am Muslim too!"

Bowtie took a step back, almost as if he had a change of plans. As soon as Rhino gathered a little bit of his strength back, he lunged forward into Bowtie like a football position. Punching him with solid, hard blows to the rib cage and hollering, "Nothing's fair, right?" The powerful tackle threw the taser right where Bowtie had setup a leg and arm trap; he was prepared. Bowtie knew Rhino was much bigger than him, so convincing him of a fair fight out was the best way to lure him into killing the strongest member out the crew.

Rhino kept punching him and continued asking questions of Serenity's whereabouts. Rhino continued, "What is Co's final plan now?" In pain taking the licks, he attempted to speak. He spit out blood saying, "they were in Miami, but leaving the next day for Argentina."

The news hitting Rhino harder and harder. He asked where could he find them in Miami, and what he planned on doing in Argentina? Bowtie smiled and simply said, "I don't know." Rhino not once believing him, sent a face shot. Boom! Bowtie's head was spinning. The only thing he could do, was attempt a move for the taser, and hope Rhino grabbed it and fell in the trap. Rhino kept punching him asking for answers, but

Bowtie kept lying saying he didn't know anything else. Rhino saw him reaching for the taser. Rhino leaped off him to grab it, and turn the tables on him, but his leg was air lifted. He hung upside down from the balcony eye level, with a standing Bowtie.

Flint knew something was wrong, because him and Serenity talked about their plan the night before. It was at least an hour passed the time, it would have took for that mission. Kicking through the front door of the address Serenity had given him, incase anything went wrong. The loud music and lights brought him straight to the courtyard. Bowtie had his pocket knife out, now demanding info on Mike and Flint. Rhino spat at him, "you might as well kill me. I'll never talk." Bowtie said, "well you know Malcom X was Muslim, and his own killed him." Then put the blade across his throat. Bok! A bullet to the back of his head that sent pieces of his brain through his forehead landing on Rhino. Flint slumped him. He died doin' dirty work.

TRIP TO FLORIDA

After loading up on the private plane that seats only eight to ten people; Flint, Rhino, Mike, Dez, Reba, and Karen were headed to Miami. They took Bowtie's phone and went through his phone calls, text messages, and notes. They learned that Bowtie was supposed to kill them, then meet at the house Co leased out, in Fort Lauderdale. Co hustled bigger and stronger now. After they killed the One Life niggas and his family; Co took the insurance money, money his mom left behind, and the money from his fucked up child. Turning it into a lucrative coke dealing business. Moving dope from South Florida to Louisiana. He was paid. He had goons around his trap spot in the pork and beans projects. Co's main hitter, Bowtie, watched the house. Going through Bowtie's phone also revealed fishy traits about Karen. One message read:

"Send message after it's done. Karen will be meeting us also. I have some dick and coke for her, lol boss shit."

Flint didn't understand where Karen came in this situation at all. He knew it was a lot of tension between Serenity and Karen, and before getting everyone together for Florida. It hit him, that the call he had seen on his phone put to Karen, wasn't by him. It was from Serenity, and maybe Karen set Serenity up, by tipping Co off. Whatever the conclusion was, Flint was gone get the business clear, and let Karen hang herself.

Landing at Miami International, the crew got a hotel connected to the airport. Dez rented a rental, and Reba rented one. Since Karen was supposed to be meeting with Bowtie and Co, he switched the original plan up, and sent Karen and Reba to check out the projects like customers. They were told to see how many men he had working, and to send word if Co popped up. The guys took the other rental and hit the interstate to the Fort Lauderdale crib. They were to stake it out, until they seen movement or got word.

All day, the girls had been going in and out the projects buying coke. Reba was sticking to the plan, but Karen was really snorting that shit. They kept Flint with the latest news. The most important thing they had learned, was all Co workers had a PB1L tatted on them. These niggas were beefed out in their own section, behind a nigga that wasn't from around there. He just had the funds.

Karen was out her mind, spilling out info to Reba. She was telling her how things were so good between her and Flint. Until that bitch, Serenity, came back home. In between sniffs, she talked about how good the dick was, and she couldn't have it all for herself. She said Serenity, and this stupid ass beef, was stopping there money also. They couldn't even work peacefully.

Reba knew her girl was relapsing. She hadn't seen her this bad, since she had the drug habit. Reba didn't know if it was Flint, or if it was the good Miami coke, that had her girl trippin'. Karen started crying, saying that this was all because of her. If she would've let business be business, and not try to mess with a man in a relationship, they wouldn't be in the state their in now. Reba was trying to console her friend, by assuring these events came before they were in the picture. That this was old beef. Karen said, "No, I set Serenity up."

There it was, the beans were spilled. Reba grabbed her from the driver seat, squeezing her and shaking her. With question after question, "What did you say? How did you? How could you?" Karen explained it all, from how scared she was to lose Flint. To the call Serenity made to her, and the call she made to Co. Reba knew they were in trouble. She put the car in drive and hollered at Karen all the way back to the hotel. She told Karen, "Now we both have toe tags waiting for us!"

The next plan was either to disappear before Flint found out or rat her girl out. She was close to Serenity and Karen, so this was going to be hard. The F-Girls were slowly fading away. The guys knew something was wrong, because it was now night time, and no one seen Co. The later it got, the more Flint worried.

ARGENTINA

From the Ocean Drive suite view, Co watched those fools searching high and low for him on his hand-held device. It was equipped with camera angles, zoom in, and an alarm system. The held hostage, Serenity, sat still while Co's son played with the newest goon on Co's team. Locka who was a young matted dread head from Opalocka. He earned the name from running his set. Locka and his crew was having problems with niggas selling for Co called the PB1's.

Co reached out to the young hitter and offered him a job. Not just any job, but one higher than the guys selling dope for him. He would roll with him and protect him. That way when Co is in town, he's good in every hood. He had the 2 main areas working for him now, and everybody was eating. The only problem was, at times there were some niggas not feeling their position. The PB1's thought a nigga direct hustling for Co, should have been his main hitter, but the truth was. Co seen, his trappers couldn't hold them niggas coming from Opalocka off. He needed the strongest and got that. They felt something wrong, when Co didn't hear from Bowtie anymore.

Even Karen hadn't contacted him. Co knew it would be only a matter of time, before Flint and company, would come tearing the beach up. Looking for his back-stabbing hoe, and unborn seed.

Co turned to Locka and told him, "I will be leaving for Argentina in the morning. I have everything taken care of. The fake passports and ID's for me, my son, and Ms. Home health care." Co was very confused, with what he truly wanted to do with Serenity. A part of him wanted to run away with her, start a life with her, and her being a mother to his child. But the other part of him knew, she was the girlfriend, and future baby mother of his enemy. That thought, made him wanna mail her piece by piece, back to the states and make him suffer before he dies.

Co gave Locka the following orders, "Clear the street, kill my beef, and run my empire while I am away. Since Bowtie can't do it maybe a younger hungrier street nigga can sit onside me at the top." Co hollered loudly and waved a gun at Serenity saying, "You get Jr. ready for bed. We have to fly out in the morning." Knowing she could possibly never come back, after getting on this next flight. She was in desperate need, of a way to get out of the suite with Co.

Locka stopped in the hood and picked up his biker boy who followed behind the rental truck on a ninja with a backpack full of ammo and a Drako. With footage from the camera, Co used the views from every angle to tell Locka what car they were in, where they were staked out at, and all. Locka left the rental truck parked a few blocks away in a vacant spot. Then, hopped on the back of the bike and crept through the suburban area.

Flint, Mike, Dez, and Rhino was getting weary. No one wanted to abort the mission, because Flint's girl was held hostage. No one knew her status, and they all had just found out she was pregnant. With a ring to Mike's phone, he shouted, "Reba is calling right now!" Flint snatched the phone, and blew on her saying, "what the fuck is wrong with you? What the fuck is up with your girl, huh?" He tried to play the game raw, by leaving her in the blind of not knowing, he knew about the setup. He thought he could bargain with them, or at least put her life on the line to save Serenity's, but nothing was working.

By the time Reba was saying, "It's all Karen's fault. She's on that stuff again." A speeding ninja firing bullets as long as fingers, and as loud as cannons, made them drop floor level in their rental journey. If it wasn't for Dez being alert as the driver, it would've been closed casket for all four of them.

Without any returned shots, they all began checking each other for bullet holes. They pushed the van that was now filled with holes and busted windows to the airport, left it, and got to the hotel. After a ten-hour flight Co, Serenity, and Jr. landed safely in Buenos- Aires Argentina. A message popped up from Locka saying:

"We cleared the streets boss."

DEATH MILES

Breaking news: The events that took place at the Stay Short Hotel, connected to Miami International Airport, was horrific. Around four o'clock a.m. two unidentified black males, opened fired on a small entourage of people, checking out of the hotel. A small hand gun, and an assault rifle, was used by the two gunmen. What looked to be like two females and two males, all black, packed to board a flight. Stunned, drew out weapons of their own, and fired back. The news reporter went on saying, an unidentified female, was pronounced dead outside of the hotel. Outside surveillance, last seen the victims, chasing the two males. Who opened fired first, before vanishing.

Crossing the Women's Bridge, in the heart of Argentina, Co couldn't believe the news clip that popped up on his phone. He couldn't get to his Spanish condo, quick enough, to call Locka.

Serenity walked with Jr. wearing shades, to hide the red eyes from crying since leaving the states and hearing the news about Locka spraying the car Flint was in. She only cheered up, when hearing the news clip on Co's phone. She put two and two together, and thought, if the news people said four people. This morning was targeted, and only one dead female was left on the scene, then Flint must still be alive. She hoped the dead female was Karen.

The plan worked fine, Flint and Mike changed clothes in the airport bathroom, before boarding the flight to Argentina. They all had decided to kill Karen. Reba didn't wanna do it personally, but she knew to save herself, and show she had nothing to do with the setup. She had to do something. Everything she had heard, she told Flint. Karen was a dead woman.

While everyone else was sleeping that night. Flint and Mike decided to act like the two shooters they came in counter with earlier. Since the PD was probably out looking for Co's shooters in the suburban neighborhood, they would assume these were the same guys. Everybody had fake ID's, passports, and tickets to Argentina. Everybody knew only Flint and Mike were going, except for Karen. When everyone woke to catch the flight, she must have sensed something wrong, because she knew everyone now knew about her betrayal. But everyone payed no attention to her. Now hustling last minute for tickets and plans to get Serenity back. When Karen asked for Flint and Mike, they told her that they went get the tickets printed out. The dumb broad fell for the okie dokie. She was riddled with bullets. Her team shot back at the air, then vanished without a trace. She was left slumped for betrayal. That bitch died doin' dirty work.

Flint gave Rhino detailed instructions He wanted pressure put on the PB1's, and whoever else, Co had dealings with in Miami. Flint knew the only way to find Serenity, was to get through Co's crew. Flint continued, "Find the person or people that was in on that Ninja hit, or start getting his money including the trap spot, the Fort Lauderdale crib, and the New Orleans crib. Rhino, turn Dez into a solid killer, and Reba too; if you have to."

The circle had to stay small and tight, if they wanted loyalty. Karen was a perfect example, of what could happen in the crew. Pressing the key to the keypad. Co said, "your little boyfriend just doesn't wanna die, huh?" His security was waiting inside the lobby and handed him the key to the 6th floor condo. The elevator ride was filled with silence. Seemed like no one wanted to be there, but Co. Jr. was too small, to fully understand what was going on.

The big wood grain door opened, and a lavish pad worth a half of million, was to comfort them. This was life, whether she liked it or not. Under any other circumstances, Serenity would've felt like she died and went to heaven. But being with this psycho kidnapper, pregnant, and thinking about Flint every second. She could never give in to Co. She would play his game to stay alive, and hope and pray, Flint could save her from his madness.

As Flint and Mike exited the plane, the sign read "Welcome to Argentina!"

Do they get Serenity back?

Find out what happens to Flint and Mike by reading

Part II of Died Doin' Dirty Work: Team – 13

Coming Soon!!!

THE SILENT THEATERS: MODERN DAY DICTATORSHIP

(SNIPPET)

MID 60'S INTRO

THE SILENT THEATERS: MODERN DAY DICTATORSHIP

(SNIPPET)

It was mid 1960's when the youngest child, Clifford Izin, of a married slave couple was born on the state line of Louisiana crossing into Mississippi. The Izin's were like most black families in that time period. Living in dark fear, poor, and living on their purchaser land. Which whom they adopted their last name from. William Izin, a powerful silver head, from the superior Izin family was born into wealth. He owned land from Slidell, Louisiana; the city where his new workers were purchased. To Bay St. Louis, Mississippi, where they were housed at.

Unlike most slave owners who split couples up, William saw strong features in this young husband and wife. He decided to keep them both. It wasn't long before Mary and Ruper started making babies. Billy was the first child, whom they named after master William's middle name. They named their middle child Wheatly, after their master's wife. All four, piled in a shotgun shack yards away from the big house. Billy was put to work by the age of ten. While little Wheatly was helping mother at age five. Even though times were hard, they were blessed with what they did have; each other. For the most part, they felt like they were treated fairly by their owners.

William Izin's dad died devoting his life to forming a superior group. Like others, he died doin' dirty work. This wasn't the KKK, they government, or anything dealing with Washington D.C. This was a citizen's organization, and decades later, it would resurface again. The great Clifford the first, whom the slaves named their youngest child after, made a name for himself in the south by forming a group based on totalitarianism. The great party included Mississippi's head lawyers, doctors, politicians, down to the teachers. Most of all, those people were living a double life. Since the police were joined in the KKK, the great Clifford used secret police, and made sure to maintain political power in the south.

Even though the head wasn't as racist as most whites, his body of people was. They started fires, lynchings, overly using nigger calling, and casting guilt behind his back. By the time blacks would complain to the powerful leader, the details and events would be covered up. And like all matters in the south during this time, nothing would be done. Over the years, the tragedies and age would catch up to him. His reign withered with the rise of the civil rights movement, and the fall of the KKK.

Before his heart failed over what would become of the new south, he shared a secret that only him, William, and Mary knew. Her last child, the youngest baby boy, was his grandchild. Indeed, he was named after the great Clifford; his only grandson. And on his dying bed, he left Cliff the shiny ticket with penned letters. That no one was to open, or read, until he was taught how to read. Receiving a proper education, just like the free people.

William Izin had been living a double life like most of his peers. See, he loved his wife, Wheatly, but he had a craving for the young African American help. That ended up over time, borning a mixed baby. In the shack, where all Mary's and Ruper's other kids were dark-skinned. This was no longer a secret. Once Ruper back handed Mary into the front yard demanding answers and making a scene. Wheatly Izin came to her rescue and couldn't understand why Ruper would be burning with anger and not celebrating the birth of his third child. His second son. She knew William would be happy it was a boy and would be ready to get him to work as soon as he could walk.

All those emotions changed once Wheatly saw the baby. Her cheerful smile turned to a worry that had very limited options. That baby was conceived by a white man, and the only white man that was on that land was her husband, "William." Who was out on the town that day checking on properties, and hoping the birth went well. Of course, wishing for it to be a boy, to now have three workers.

Entering the big house, William was very surprise to find a broken wife weeping by the fire place. He grabbed her hand and kneeled by her asking what was wrong. He shook her until she muttered some words off, "I can't believe you, I can't believe you did this. To me, to yourself, to this community, to what we stand for." All he kept saying was, "Baby what is it?!" She brought herself to say, "All I've asked, is you don't touch those dirty nigger whores, and you go and bare a child with our help." The last words, before she went up to the master bedroom and locked the doors stung. She softly, with anger said, "Now you have to take care of that nigger Ruper, and if I have to see that Dalmation child, or Mary again. I'll take care of it myself."

Ruper had already knew the scene he caused earlier that day, and a white family's pride would result in his death. A stick bag packed and running through the woods came to a quick holt. With a lake in front of him, barking dogs, an old Chevy truck, and a long riffle sticking out. A look at the lake, then a quick look at the riffle, he decided to jump in; but his decision was a tad bit too late. The right side of Ruper head was blown off. The only thing that would reach the water was his ear.

Back at the shotgun shack, a crying Mary sat in her little kitchen caring for her newborn while her oldest and middle child slept in their only bedroom. Mary knew what was to come from all of this, but she fantasied William protecting her. Even though his wife was humiliated. Even though she knew it was over with between her and Ruper, she still loved him and wanted him to make it out safe. Mary was in deep thought when she heard the cracking sounds of her door being opened. As she sat the baby down to make a move to check it out, check mate. She was strangled in front her crying baby until the veins in her eyes popped out, and she no longer existed.

With her two kids still sleeping, and a unnurtured baby laying in the kitchen, Mary's body was thrown in the back of the old Chevy with Ruper's. Hauled off, back to the same lake on property. Legs cemented bound together like their marriage, and sunken down below.

William Izin hated the slaughter he had hours ago approved. Even though white men had been sleeping with black women, it was not to be publicized, and God forbid the wife finds out or suspects it. The nigger whore would either be sold or at worst killed. "This was just the only way; they could cope with such a thing."

Black men had a lot of white women throwing themselves at them. Especially during the civil rights movement. They would come down south to help protest, demonstrate, and find themselves falling in love. With a southern boy, the backlash of course came from the public. Most of all from the woman's parents, she would be outed as a nigger lover. "This was just the only way; they could cope with such a thing."

William sat in his study all night reflecting on everything. His love for his wife, and his love affair with the young African American woman whom he bore a child with. By middle of the night, William had come up with a plan. His action would change lives of people in a way him or his dad, the great Clifford, could have never imagined. He had no other choice, but to split the two kids up.

He sent Billy to a slave auction in Georgia, and little Wheatly, to a slave auction in Alabama.

To keep their status in the public eye, he had little Clifford sent to a freed African American family in Louisiana. In which he paid a pretty penny to have him receive the best education the state had to offer. He wanted frequent reports on the boy. That was his only two concerns; no visits, and to no circumstances must he know his family history.

William purchased another family, moved them in the vacant shotgun shack, and started life over. Filled with hurt, over letting go the only son he would ever have.

MODERN DAY CLIFF

THE SILENT THEATERS: MODERN DAY DICTATORSHIP

(SNIPPET)

A very successful businessman sat behind his desk at a Government Street loaning center located in south Baton Rouge. The wavy haired, almond skinned, ripped money handler was a site to see behind the thick glass. Women would stop in to pay bills, get a loan, and send money orders out to their loved ones in jail. Men would stop and get a throw away card for their pimpin' and mostly sending Western Unions to drug cartels.

Clifford Izin now in his early forty's, not looking a day over thirty, reflected on his childhood while watching a frequent customer "Wright Wade" walk out the door after a transaction. Cliff knew how it felt to be young and lost. He remembered not fitting in with the neighborhood black kids, because he wasn't black enough. At school he didn't fit in with the white kids, because he wasn't white enough. His mother and father, Rodney and Lily Raines, always assured him to be himself; to choose his own identity and be the best student in the school.

Even though he had a lot of challenges, he found comfort in his school work and of course in the house of the Lord. Which is where all three went every Sunday. As a young boy, he loved Math and he played number games with the kids and grownups. He always came out on top. No one from his childhood was surprise that the young Clifford had his hands in money loaning, pre-paid cards, and bill paying.

A tragedy hurricane would soon hit and his smarts paid off for him tremendously. In 2005, Hurricane Katrina hit the coast of Mississippi and destroyed New Orleans. Yes, a lot of residents moved to Houston but a lot of short travelers went forty-five minutes west to Baton Rouge. Cliff now had more customers getting loans and sending money out than ever before. Between 2005 – 2006 his numbers were showing him, he was in the right business. At the right time.

He was so ecstatic, he had longer conversations with customers. Even going as far as asking them their plans, and ideas on business establishments. Of course, the neighborhood girls throughout ideas of hair and nail salons. Some older women, even men, said restaurant chains. A lot of the young thugs said clubs, strip clubs, any and everything clubs. Two people's ideas, an evacuee from Waveland, Mississippi; "Norman Hangs." And also a familiar face at Cliff's, Wright Wade, who was always in the city hustling. But now living there due to being flooded out in New Orleans.

Norman Hangs, the fifty-year-old husband with twin daughters. Suggested he'd run a church. He already went to school to become a pastor, he just hit hard times. With being the only provider of the household, while his wife Anne cared for the little girls. Being a correctional officer wasn't making it, and that's why he was in the city getting a loan today.

Wright Wade's idea was a record label. He made it sound real good too. Enticing Cliff with names of R&B and rap artist that signed with independent record labels before landing major deals. Cliff couldn't believe some of his favorite artist started with ten to twenty thousand dollars. But in some cases, much less. The main things that concerned him with this idea, was the local artist he heard about blowing up; Such as, Lil Boosie. Was a risk, meaning involved in drugs and violence. He figured if he didn't make his way to jail or the grave, he'll leave the independent label for his own or more dollars somewhere else.

Wright assured him saying, "Yes, there are the main problems, but by you being a businessman; you would have your paperwork right. You'll make enough money to live comfortable and be off to the next act before shit hits the fan." Cliff and Wright Wade chopped it up, until the end of his shift. Wright was sure the money man would be in contact with him, about some further inquiries.

That night while Cliff sat in his all white loft surrounded by glass over looking College

Drive, he pulled out his latest Apple laptop and did a ton of research on church ownership, and CEO's of startup record labels. Doing number estimates, locations, and licensing permits until early morning. He knew the toughest tasks would be knowing he got the correct people to go in business with.

He kept information on all his clients so now he would play them close, feel them out but keep the two businesses and people separate. Cliff knew church was God's playground, and he loved church coming up. He seen the money benefits that came from it while giving back to the community. Music could be the devil's playground. But what he didn't know was even though one was white and one was black, they would be more alike then he could imagine.

HANGS

THE SILENT THEATERS: MODERN DAY DICTATORSHIP

(SNIPPET)

Just two years ago, Norman Hangs was following the steps of his father who followed steps of a generation before him, being a state police officer. After being trained since a young boy of how to terrorize the county's of Mississippi, it was time to get sworn in. Hangs was on the force for twenty-eight years, before his dirt really caught up to him.

In 1965, he was a little boy riding shotgun in an old Chevy pickup truck. With his drunk policeman dad firing shots from both sides of the vehicle, to see who could hit the black target. At this time, Norman was in training, but George Hangs was a professional at hitting targets. If they still moved after a perfect shot, he'd hang them wherever with whatever he had. His bring along son would only ask his father, "Why kill an innocent man?!" His father would answer straight forward and hard, "He's black he's always wrong, white is right, black is fright. We hate those niggers... right son?!" "Yes, sir pops!"

George patrolled in uniform during the day and worked as a secret officer at night. For a citizens organization formed by the Great Clifford the first. Their main goals were to control their community with cultural, social, and political power. Of course, a lot of racism was going on behind closed doors, but George specialized in taking out the slaves that needed a lesson. It was an honor to help his leader's son reconcile his life with his wife by taking out the slave couple. Who was better to bring on the journey than his cub in training, his son. Norman could still remember telling his dad, "I did it, I did it. I knocked off it's ear." Even though he stayed in the truck during the strangling of Mary, he never forgot the sound of the cement and bodies hitting the water.

Norman reflected on his life and catching his first body, while sitting in a packed courthouse. Alongside his wife Sherri, and college twin daughters, Kristi and Kary. They came to support him along with other members of the force. Former officer Norman Hangs followed two black guys into a no trespassing area and stopped them for a search and seizure. But when he couldn't find nothing, he withdrew a hot 9mm. Shot the driver in the chest, then shot the passenger in the head. With a planted gun in the passenger hand, and a hot 9mm in the driver hand. This looked like a drug deal gone bad, in the middle of the night. That left both slumped with a pile of drugs left behind.

Because Hangs was the first to respond to such a tragedy, he had to speak what he witnessed upon arriving to the crime scene. While no one questioned his statement, speculation spread through the community that those two boys frequently met up with his twin girls at a friend's house to smoke and sex. It didn't stop there, they even kept in touch while in college and continued having affairs. Kristi and Kary couldn't come with questioning their providing father, but deep down inside they knew he had a hand in the murders. Because of a lot of complaints from the black community the department had no choice but to remove the forty-eight year old from patrol duty, and activate him as a Mississippi county correctional officer.

The move from patrolling the streets to controlling the walk was a big difference. It was a little slow, but Hangs would still make it action packed. In his first week at MCJ, he locked twenty black inmates up in the blocks for simple write ups and from picking fights so him and other C.O,'s could pound on one inmate. His name spread throughout the jail as someone to try and avoid by all means. It wasn't long before they started finding out from the outside world who this guy was and what he stood for. The inmates knew his family history, and his acquittal from slaying two innocent black guys. The big question was, why wasn't this guy locked up in the county, instead of running the county? The reality was, they all knew this country was built on white, and whites' rule.

Most of the rank running the system, were murderers while the minority inmates were majority drug offenders doing maximum sentence. Most of the faces there were repeat offenders or had been in the system a decade long. Even though the controllers changed laws for non-violent offenders, most of the inmates due to living circumstances. Would find their way back to stripes and jumpsuits.

The sad part was, the C.O's knew this. They ate and fed their families by keeping the jailhouse packed. Even though Hangs didn't see eye to eye with blacks, he secretly admired the way they hustled and how creative and talented they were. He just laughed at the fact that they wouldn't amount to anything, because they would always go backwards to the pin instead of forward to corporations.

Hangs played mind games all the time with the inmates. If you was big and bad, he'd pick with you around other C.O's so they could get the best of you; if you crashed out. If you were a worker trying to better yourself, he'd catch you alone and drive you with meaningless discipline. About a bag your carrying or the clothes your wearing. Just to make you react so he can threaten to take your job and lock you up in the blocks. Because he can.

This one inmate in particular, for some reason, always crossed Hangs path every morning. It was always spiteful shots spat at the eighteen-year-old teenager, but he always brushed it off. Kept his head high, and kept it moving. Hangs motive was to get the guy to click and flash out on him. Partly because he was young, and Hangs hated young thugs. The other part was, because the young man had a job and was going to school to better himself.

While the other inmates his age, stayed in the cells taking drugs, or in the blocks on disciplinary. Hangs hated to be out smarted, so he stayed on the young man trail. He would go as far as turning the inmate around in the cold after a mile walk from the unit, to change uniforms on test days. And if it's also store day, he'd make the guy bring his store bag back to the unit to make him late for his test, while letting all the white inmates proceed along with their bags on the walk. To avoid violations, the inmate would comply because he saw the bigger picture of getting out. He was only serving two and some change off a petty drug charge. He hated the fact that he had crossed the state line with anything on him knowing how those crooked motherfuckers were.

With this bid almost behind him and getting his GED. The only words escaped his mouth, to the stalking cop was, you suppose to love all God's children. The issue with that was, all the rank down to the C.O's, claimed Christianity. But no one upheld the teachings. Even though Hangs wouldn't admit this out loud. It stung him to hear this, out of a little ghetto boy mouth. Out of all the inmates Hangs had confrontation with, not one of them had spoke of God, and he reflected on how far gone he had gotten. From his studies at the college.

From that moment on, Hangs never acknowledged the boy, or looked in his direction again. But most of all, the harassment stopped. The teen got his certificate, and was back in the streets, before anyone missed him. Norman tried praying, and walking with a different approach on the compound, but the terror he inflicted on that prison. Was much too thick, to just one day tell over nine hundred inmates. I've been saved by the Lord again, and I will treat all of you equal. So instead, he just let his work ethic speak for itself, he stayed out of peoples way. Gave more rec time, left the showers open for anytime use, and from time to time. Gave treats to workers and school goers.

Battling his past, his religion, and being the provider for his family. He knew the position of a C.O. wouldn't fund his life, and he could easily move up to rank, but how would this change his life and other peoples lives? He needed a new start, the church, his own church. But he would need money, sponsoring, and major help. To have the right people join, instead of a church house full of evil. Meeting up, to do the same things he's already done. He made a memo to meet with some loaning companies, and for some reason. He wanted to check up on the teenager, that left life changing words, behind with him.

Died Doin' Dirty Work: From the Dump

THE SILENT THEATERS: MODERNDAY DICTATORSHIP

Coming Soon!

Josh is currently incarcerated in Louisiana finishing his sentence, and working on his Associate's Degree.

Note From the Author:

It is very important that I hear from my readers, I appreciate each and every one of you. If you enjoyed reading this book, please consider writing a review and rating it on Amazon. Thank you!

Printed in the USA
CPSIA information can be obtained
at www.ICGtesting.com
LVHW091046190224
772230LV00007B/99